HAIRBAG NATION

A Story of the New York City Transit Police

Book 1

The Police Riot

Robert L. Bryan

D1519790

For Meghan – Always in my Heart.

CONTENTS

PROLOGUE

A long time ago in a city far, far away known as New York, there existed turmoil and strife. Crime had gripped the land and while the council of the city endlessly debated the escalating chaos, the people suffered. Out of the fog of unrest emerged a force for good. This force was called the police, and they would battle to take the streets back from the evil that had taken hold. But the evil was not limited to the streets. Crime and chaos had also taken seized the city's subterranean underworld. The citizenry quaked in fear at the thought of descending into the dark, dank subways. In this hour of need, new heroes came forth – a special force known as the transit police would battle the underground evil to take back the subways for the people. The battle for the underworld was not without cost. An evil sorcerer cast a spell on the transit police. Some of the officers were immune to the spell, but many fell victim to the magic and were transformed. Their consciousness was altered into the antithesis of what their leaders told them a member of the force should be. They became lazy, cynical, contemptuous, apathetic, and indifferent. In short, they were transformed into hairbags. This is their tragic story. This is hairbag nation.

●●●

I don't remember exactly when I heard the word "hairbag" for the first time. I believe it may have been when an instructor addressed my class during the waning days of my police academy training.

"Remember what you've learned over the last six months." he said. "Don't pick up bad habits from all the hairbags out there."

With that initial warning, hairbag became a standard part of my vocabulary. So, what exactly is a hairbag? My interest in its origin was recently piqued when I read an article about a lawsuit underway in New York City. A member of the NYPD had initiated the action because he claimed his career had been adversely impacted because his boss referred to him as a hairbag. I'll be very interested to see how that case turns out because it may finally provide a legal definition for the term.

The origin and meaning of hairbag has always been somewhat hazy. For as long as anyone can remember, younger officers in the police departments in New York City have referred to their elders as hairbags — usually behind their backs. It's an archaic bit of slang with obscure origins. In police parlance, "the bag" means "the uniform." So, some officers believe hairbag is a riff on a longtime officer's uniform — so old it has become hairy — and describes veterans who know what the police call "The Job" inside out. This seems to be the most positive spin on the expression. Others think the phrase is an insult that comes from the practice, perhaps apocryphal, of officers using a haircut as an excuse for leaving their posts. This theory holds that sergeants used to demand a bag of hair trimmings as proof, and eventually burned-out officers who shirked work came to be known as hairbags.

I came to know a hairbag as an older cop - a burned-out cop, who didn't want to do anything and didn't care anymore. Another possibility is that the word traces its roots to the Fire Department, not the Police Department. A retired New York City fire chief explained in a magazine article that as far back as the 19th century, firefighters would use a haircut as an excuse to leave the firehouse, sometimes for a romantic tryst. He said that firefighters who missed an alarm for a fire while supposedly out getting a haircut would be labeled as hairbags.

The word has been used in the Police Department since at least 1958, when it appeared in a glossary of "New York City Police Argot" in the department's magazine, Spring 3100. The definition was brief and neutral: a veteran policeman. A 1970 article in The New York Times gave the word a more positive spin, defining a hairbag as "a veteran patrolman with backbone."

Over time, it appears, the word took on the more negative connotation of a bitter and burned-out complainer who shirks his duties. What is for sure is that the phrase shows no sign of dying out and is ingrained in the police lexicon. In fact, I recently discovered that a satirical website called the Hairbag Times was established in 2017.

So, back to the original question. What is a hairbag? Is a hairbag simply a veteran cop with a wealth of knowledge and experience, or is it a cop who does nothing except come to work, read the paper, eat meals, shit, sleep, wake up and then go home - usually a slob who complains about everything everybody else is doing, is not reliable in a tense situation, and is probably hiding somewhere while everyone else is breaking their ass. Personally, I'll go with the latter definition.

One final thought. This book is a tongue in cheek fictitious account of a segment of the policing world set many years ago. I can't begin to imagine how this twisted society is affecting the mindset of police officers all over the country. Society seems to have flipped with the new order dictating that the cops are the lowlifes and the lowlifes are to be celebrated. Add in a generous portion of gutless leadership and it is no wonder that cops end up doing as little as possible on patrol.

So, are hairbags born or are they a byproduct of the stresses of the job? I'm not sure. I'll leave that answer to people much smarter than me. What do you think? What I would say to all my brothers and sisters in blue who are still out there doing their jobs in the midst of the insanity – stay strong and stay safe!

Robert L. Bryan

INTRODUCTION

Queens Criminal Court: 1983

The only sound was his footsteps crossing the polished wood floor. He made his way to the witness stand like he had walked the walk a thousand times before. His gait was one of extreme confidence, bordering on arrogance. Every hair was in place and his Pierre Cardin suit accentuated his athletic physique perfectly for the spectators in the packed courtroom. A quick wink at the pretty, rapidly blushing court reporter was followed by a nod of acknowledgement to the judge just before he lowered himself into the creaking witness chair.

In an environment that brought many to tears, he was completely at ease. He smiled suggestively at the attractive 35-year old assistant district attorney who obviously was falling victim to his charm when her papers flew out of her folder and floated to the floor on both sides of the podium. The prosecutor regained her papers and composure and took a deep breath behind the podium.

"Good afternoon, officer."

"Good afternoon, ma'am," he smiled.

"Would you please state your name for the record, officer."

"Angelo Petrino." He spelled his last name like an experienced witness would know to do. "P-E-T-R-I-N-O"

"Thank you," The prosecutor replied. "And would you tell the court your current rank."

"Police officer."

"For what department?"

"The New York City Transit Police Department, ma'am."

"And how long have you been a police officer?"

"Six hours."

•••

In the middle of the nineteenth century, two rival police forces were operating at the same time in one major U.S. city—it did not end well. In April 1857, the State Legislature passed a law which disbanded New York's Municipal Police, ostensibly for corruption and to enforce liquor laws, and replaced it with a State-controlled Metropolitan Police force that encompassed the area of Manhattan, then independent Brooklyn, Staten Island, and Westchester County. The mayor of New York City claimed the new police force was illegal since it violated the principle of home rule and sued. A decision would not be made for months. In the meantime, the mayor's Municipal force and the State's

11

Metropolitans were operating in the same city at the same time.

With the stage set for conflict, the two forces often competed with each other. In one instance, for example, a man arrested for drunken and disorderly conduct refused to recognize the Metropolitans arresting him as officers and only gave himself up when a Municipal came on the scene. This resulted in a nasty melee between the two forces and a near riot.

In June of 1857 the governor of New York obtained an arrest warrant for the mayor of New York City and directed the state-run metropolitans to arrest the mayor. The mayor, holding his staff of office, refused to recognize the jurisdiction of the Metropolitans.

At 3:30 pm, a phalanx of 50 Metropolitans marching two abreast entered City Hall Park. The Metropolitans were in full uniform with frock coats and newly minted badges. Each of their plug hats was decorated with a ribbon labeled "Metropolitan Police" and their officer number. They brandished batons— nearly 12-inch clubs which were their primary tools for law enforcement.

The Metropolitans attempted to enter City Hall to seize the mayor, but an overwhelming force of Municipal Police arrived on the scene and attacked the Metropolitans.

The Metropolitans fled the field with the Municipals and a mob chasing after them. An estimated 53 officers from both police forces were injured in the riot. The mayor's Municipal Police were finally disbanded when the New York Court of Appeals ruled in the State's favor leaving the Metropolitan Police as the sole police agency in New York City.

In 1984, three police departments operated independently in New York City. The New York City Police Department had evolved from the Metropolitan Police Force, but in the middle part of the twentieth century transit and housing police departments were established to police the subways and public housing projects, respectively.

In 1995 the transit and housing forces were merged into the NYPD, once again leaving a single police department to police New York City. While the three agencies exited, professional rivalries developed, but generally the departments cooperated well in policing the city. It didn't seem realistic that there could ever be another police riot. Every now and then, however, there were flashbacks to 1857 and the Municipals and Metropolitans. Such was the case in 1984.

THE ROLL CALL

Summer, 1984:
New York City Transit Police Headquarters
370 Jay Street, Brooklyn
Wednesday: 11:00 am

Every now and then George Hall reverted to his most basic emotion – anger. There were times in his life when George lived in anger, almost as cartoon characters do, so lost in that moment and the torment his brain was in. It would be visible in his eyes first, then his muscles would tense and an inability to think clearly soon followed.

The rational Deputy Chief George Hall was offline and the primitive Police Officer Hall who terrorized miscreants in the Times Square subway decades earlier was in the room. Suddenly his liberal opinions and understanding of police professionalism were gone, along with his ability for nuance and emotional maturity. His knuckles were white from clenching his fists too hard, and he gritted his teeth from an effort to remain silent, his hunched form exuding an animosity that was like acid - burning, slicing, potent. His face was red with suppressed rage. What he wanted most at that moment was to reach out and throttle the pencil neck of Captain Arnold Morris in his huge hands. But Morris was a borough away. He glared across his office to the other desk in the room. Police Officer Herbert Dowdle typed frantically

14

at a pace to make his high school typing teacher proud. Chief Hall allowed himself a slight sadistic smile. He may not be able to reach Captain Morris, but the pencil neck of his obedient man-servant was available, and might be just as satisfying.

Chief Hall detested almost everything about Herby Dowdle. He hated the fact that he was short, thin, pale and sweated excessively. He hated the fact that he was a shameless ass kisser who would do anything to maintain his good standing in the chief's office. Most of all, Chief Hall hated the fact that Herby had been on the job for three years and had not worked a day on patrol.

Police Officer Herby Dowdle sprained his ankle during his academy graduation when he fell off the stage at Brooklyn College after shaking hands with the Chief of the Department. He managed to milk that ankle injury for a year in restricted duty status. He was sent to the Chief of Patrol's office where he quickly became such an administrative asset that when he was finally forced to return to full duty status, the former Chief of Patrol had no choice but to keep him in the office. Herby had now been Chief Hall's serf for a little more than a year, and the chief quickly recognized how essential Herby was to the efficient operation of the office. Recognizing Herby's importance didn't mean he couldn't despise him.

Chief Hall quickly embarked on a campaign of humiliation and emasculation, the goal of which was to see how low this worm would sink to escape patrol. Sending Herby out to get his lunch was child's play for a professional ass kisser. Herby never batted an eye when the chief handed him his shoes with the order to give then a good old-fashioned spit shine. When no pride or self-esteem appeared, the chief turned up the dial further by having Herby kneel in front of him and shine his shoes while they were on his feet. When a rare feeling of guilt would manage to sneak into his brain, the chief would quickly justify his humiliation of Herby. As a black man whose ancestors had endured hundreds of years of slavery, his abuse of pasty faced Herby Dowdle was his personal reparations. Even providing Herby a feather duster and directing him to dust the office elicited not an inkling of a negative response. The chief was considering calling Herby into the bathroom with orders to wipe his ass, but even he wasn't sure if that was a line he should cross. Still, as he watched his pathetic worm typing at break-neck speed, he was well aware that he needed Herby Dowdle in his office, no matter how much he loathed him.

Much of Chief Hall's opinion of Herby stemmed from the fact that he was the antithesis of his assistant. Herby Dowdle was petrified of the prospect of patrol, while George Hall was born to be a patrol cop.

For ten years George Hall and Pete "Iron Head" O'Malley were partners on the Times Square complex. During that decade, while crime raged in New York City, it was almost non-existent in the Times Square subway. Even the most ambitious gangsters and gang bangers thought twice about tangling with the huge duo patrolling "The Deuce." They would much rather deal with the handcuffs of the NYPD in the street, than with subway justice issued by George and Iron Head inside a subway pipe room.

Inspector Thomas Cody was the commanding officer of District 1 during the era when George and Iron Head were the commandants of Times Square. When the inspector was transferred to headquarters and charged with the responsibility to professionalize the Transit Police Department, he recognized the potential in his Times Square team.

The NYPD mandated that the transit police stop relying on them for some specialized police functions, and to create their own specialized units, including a civilian complaint unit. Like divine inspiration, the light bulb illuminated over the inspector's head. George Hall and Iron Head O'Malley would be perfect as the Transit Police Department's first civilian complain unit. Their mission was simple. Call the people making complaints against transit police officers and make appointments to go interview them regarding their complaints. At the interview, George and Iron Head would beat the hell out of the complainant until he agreed to withdraw the complaint. As far as Inspector Cody was concerned, it was a classic case of square pegs in square holes.

Pummeling complainants into submission was a lifetime ago. George Hall had become a civilized man. He was a progressive, intelligent Chief of Patrol who recognized the essential nature of the professional policing model – most of the time. As he glared at the New York Post headline taunting him, there was no way that Times Square George was not going to make an appearance.

"Aren't you finished yet, you asshole?" George snarled.

"I apologize Chief," Herby groveled, despite the fact that he was typing at least eighty words a minute. "I'll be done in thirty seconds."

Herby ripped the sheet out of the typewriter and sprinted to the chief's desk. "Here you are, boss."

George put on his reading glasses and examined the document sitting in front of him. No matter how hard he tried to concentrate his eyes kept returning to the bold newspaper headline – *POLICE RIOT IN UNION SQUARE PARK.* He crumpled the newspaper in his massive right hand and threw it in Herby's face. The paper exploded into fifty-five different pages and floated to the floor all over the office.

"Clean that up!" George bellowed.

Herby was already on his hands and knees scurrying along the floor. "Yes, sir. It will be cleaned up in a jiffy."

Without the headline as a distraction Chief Hall could concentrate on the report prepared by his flunkie. The phone ringing on the other desk provided yet another distraction to his concentration.

"Answer that phone, god dammit!"

With globs of newspapers in both hands Herby crawled across the linoleum floor and grabbed his phone for a breathless greeting. "Chief of Patrol's Office – Police Officer Dowdle – How may I help you." Herby's eyes widened. "Yes sir. Right away sir!" His index finger pounded the hold button. "It's Chief Lawson. He wants to talk to you."

George Hall rubbed his forehead while he waited for Herby to transfer the call. This day was just getting better and better.

Politically connected Deputy Chief Thomas Lawson had been a thirty-year NYPD veteran when he was tapped to become the Chief of the Transit Police Department. During the two years of his tenure as chief, Lawson did not attempt to hide his disdain for career transit cops, considering them inferior to NYPD officers. In fact, his one big initiative as chief was to try to change the transit police uniforms so that transit cops would not be mistaken for real police officers. Bright orange uniforms were the chief's attire of choice, and only the threat of a walkout by every uniformed member of the transit police put the idea on ice.

"What the hell happened out there, Hall?"

"The facts are still being compiled, chief. I have a preliminary list of the cops who were positively identified as being present."

"I don't just want names – I want facts, and you better get the story of what happened out there!" CLICK

"Asshole!" George sneered.

"Sorry, sir," Herby cowered.

"Not you!" George stopped and corrected himself. "You are an asshole, but in this case, I happened to be referring to the asshole chief of this department."

Herby seemed relieved. "Oh, thank you very much, chief."

George picked up the report and studied the list of names. His thick index finger landed on the third name on the list – *Sgt. L. Eckhart.*

The chief dug his finger into the paper and twisted, in the same manner that he would crush a bug.

"It's that little shit dwarf Eckhart who started all this with his god damn conventions. If that dipshit Morris had done his job and put a stop to it, I wouldn't have to stare at that headline!"

Herby Dowdle picked up the last page of newspaper from the floor. "You're one hundred percent right chief. When you're right – you're right."

"Of course, I'm right," the chief bellowed. "I don't need you to tell me that!". He dropped the paper back on his desk. "Ok, asshole, get me that asshole Captain Morris on the phone."

"Yes sir!"

George shook his head. "The entire world is filled with assholes."

New York City Transit Police, District 4
Union Square, Manhattan
Tuesday: 3:30 pm

Ron Kelly cursed under his breath as he grabbed the roll call clipboard off the peg on the wall behind the desk officer. There was nothing about this task that prompted the profanity. Sgt. Kelly had been conducting roll calls on the 4 x 12 tour at District 4 for ten of his fifteen years on the job. What had Kelly agitated was the second clipboard that had only recently found a home on the same wall.

From his desk officer position, Lieutenant Steve Jankowsi sensed Ron's distress. "What's the matter with you?" he asked.

Ron waved his free hand dismissively. "Hey, Lou. Does Certs have to hold a formal roll call at the same time I'm turning out the third platoon?"

Lt. Jankowsi extended his arms with his palms up. "What can I tell you. TPF is working 4 x 12s now and they are entitled to hold roll calls just like you – deal with it!"

Ron Kelly and Larry Eckhart had graduated from the same police academy class fifteen years earlier. Ron made sergeant ten years ago while Eckhart was promoted a little less than two years ago. In 1982 the Transit Police Department had reinstituted the Tactical Patrol Force, an impressive sounding unit which in reality was used to place cops on trains from 8pm to 4am every night. It was the rookies who drew the TPF assignments as well as the rookie sergeants. Every Transit Police district had a TPF unit assigned and Sgt. Larry "Certs" Eckhart was assigned to supervise TPF in District 4.

Most of the cops believed Sgt. Eckhart's nickname was a reflection on his breath and was a reference to the popular breath mint of the day. The almost universal acceptance of this explanation was due at least in part to Larry's willingness to promote and circulate the story himself. Why would he readily concede a condition of halitosis? Larry Eckhart wanted as few people as possible to know the real genesis of his nickname.

The diminutive Sgt. Eckhart had joined the Transit Police Department during the era when there was a 5-foot 8-inch height requirement for police officers. This created a serious problem for a man 5-feet 6-inches tall. Rather than give up on his dream of being a police officer, Larry hatched a scheme. He realized that on the day of his medical examination, he would be required to remove his shoes when his official height was being recorded, but he was counting on not being required to remove his socks. He placed two one-inch inserts inside each sock, allowing the top of his head to just graze the required bar. Larry said nothing about his scam for his entire one-year probation period. Whenever a comment about his height was made, and to his great chagrin there were many of them, he would simply shrug and swear that he was 5-feet 8-inches.

Shortly after his probation period ended, Larry's academy class held an end of probation party where Larry proceeded to get extremely intoxicated and revealed to the attendees his scam using the inserts. From that day forward, he became known as Certs, not because of the breath mints, but because of the inserts he used under his socks.

As time went on Larry became paranoid that he could still get in trouble if his scheme was heard by the wrong people, so when cops began to assume the nickname was based on his bad breath, he happily admitted that his breath was horrible.

Sgt. Certs Eckhart was built for the Tactical Patrol Force. He could care less about the horrendous hours. In TPF. He was given a squad of wide-eyed rookies who were chomping at the bit to worship a hero, and who would pay no mind to the short stature of a hard charging sergeant who was also a wounded war hero.

Larry Eckhart was an Army veteran who had received the Purple Heart, fertile ground for hero worship. Just as with his nickname, however, below the surface lay a much different story than what his military exploits appeared to be. Certs never lied about his military record. To the contrary, he was always very precise when explaining that he won his Purple Heart during the Viet Nam era. What that meant was that Certs had not been to Viet Nam. He had never even been out of the country.

Larry Eckhart joined the National Guard in 1968 to avoid the possibility of being drafted and shipped to Viet Nam. In 1970 an 8-day postal strike began in New York City. Larry's Guard unit was immediately activated to perform postal duties. During his second day working at the main Manhattan Post Office, Larry was struck on the head by an errantly thrown mailbag and had to be transported to an emergency room for treatment for a concussion. Some bureaucratic pencil pusher at the Department of Defense mistook Larry's active duty mailbag hit for a combat wound and processed him for a Purple Heart. Larry accepted the commendation and never said a word.

Certs Eckhart was the undisputed monarch of his TPF squad. Billy Normile tagged his band of rookies as the Hitler youth, a nickname that caught fire within District 4, much to the displeasure of Certs Eckhart. If Certs wasn't happy with the storm trooper comparison, he certainly didn't do anything to dissuade it. He required his TPF squad to wear their full dress uniforms every tour. This included the summer blouse and white gloves that were usually reserved only for formal ceremonies. His squad did not receive much attention while they were spread out all over the city riding late night trains. It was during the T.O.M.S operations that his unit took on the look of a 1936 Munich rally.

T.O.M.S. stood for Train Order Maintenance Sweep. Every night at an appointed time, the entire squad would rendezvous with Certs at a high-profile station to conduct the TOMS. In a highly militaristic manner, Certs would line his white gloved troops up on the platform at attention and perform a meticulous inspection. At the conclusion of the inspection he would shout "Squad post!" which always sounded amplified as his voice echoed throughout the usually empty late-night station. The troops would silently march to a location on the platform so that each cop could inspect a car of an incoming train. They would silently stand at the military position of parade rest until a train arrived. When the doors opened Certs would blow his whistle as the signal for the cops to enter their assigned car. Violators of all transit rules, no matter how minor, were removed from the train and issued summonses. This included threats to the civilized world such as having an open beverage container in the car or riding with feet up on the seats. Uncooperative violators were handled in a manner that Certs very proudly named *The White Glove Treatment.*

Certs loved running his own little empire. No one screwed with him because of the TPF hours. When his squad came on duty at 8pm, the standard 3rd platoon was already four hours old. TPF units were housed in the districts but managed by the Tactical Patrol Force command staff that worked out of Transit Police headquarters at 370 Jay Street, in Brooklyn. The higher ranking TPF supervisors rarely worked the late night TPF hours, and the District 4 supervisors were very quick to point out that Certs Eckhart and his commandos were not under their jurisdiction. As a result, Certs had a free reign to terrorize the subway system nightly. Recently, however, a new wrinkle in TPF operations had threatened to upset the status quo of TPF's peaceful co-existence at District 4. After an analysis of recent crime trends, the TPF hours at District 4 were changed from 8pm x 4am to 4pm x 12am. Certs' goon squad would now be sharing the entire shift with the District 4 3rd platoon, and controversy had already erupted regarding who had priority in conducting roll call in the muster room.

It was Certs' need for rookie adoration that was the driving force behind the convention. When a small army of twenty-something cops went off duty at 4am in all corners of the city, there weren't many places they could go to unwind other than a few unsavory joints where a knock on a locked door was met with bloodshot eyes appearing in a small slot and a request for a password.

At least outwardly, Certs convinced himself that he was doing the right thing for the TPF rookies by providing them an after-work alternative to the illegal social clubs. The convention started in Central Park in the vicinity of District 1. Every night approximately one hundred members of the tactical patrol force would converge on the park after 4am to socialize, drink beer, and swap tales of life in TPF. Certs was the only sergeant attending the conventions, and the gatherings ultimately ended up with the masses circled around Certs as he told tales of the exploits of his white glove squad. The scene was very much like a Boy Scout leader sitting next to a campfire telling ghost stories to the attentive scouts. Every TPF cop wanted to get into Certs' unit and Certs loved it.

The first blow to the Certs Eckhart love fest was dealt by Manhattan's high society. The nightly conventions became rather loud, and well within earshot of the super-rich Manhattanites occupying the exclusive condos on Central Park West. Inspector Pascuale DiGenero, the gray haired, 62-year old commanding officer of the Tactical Patrol Force ordered Certs to his office at Jay Street where he pounded his desk with his fist no less than four times in forbidding Certs from holding any more off duty gatherings in Central Park. Certs departed his scolding undeterred. The inspector had specifically told him to cease the conventions in Central Park. He didn't say anything about continuing the events anywhere else.

Within a week Union Square Park, which sat directly above the Union Square subway station and District 4, became the new home of the TPF nightly conventions. There were no residential apartment buildings in the area to prompt complaints and Captain Morris was surely not going to get involved in TPF business that didn't concern him. Inspector DiGenero's warning did manage to thin the convention herd. A sizeable amount of the young TPF cops were too frightened to attend anymore. All of Certs' District 4 TPF squad still attended nightly, but they were usually supplemented by only a sprinkling of TPF cops from the rest of the city.

The shift in TPF hours created a subtle change in the conventions that would ultimately have drastic repercussions. Since TPF worked 4 x 12, the conventions were beginning in the park at midnight, at the same time the District 4 3rd platoon went off duty. It took all of about one day for the District 4 personnel on the way to their cars to realize there was a party taking place inside the park. In an instant, many members of the District 4 3rd platoon became regular convention attendees and made up for some of the waning TPF attendance.

Angelo Petrino admired his figure in the full-length mirror in the corner of the muster room and nodded in approval. Why shouldn't he? After all, he cut a dashing figure with his custom-made uniform shirt fitting perfectly over his muscular athletic physique. He moved up close to the mirror and removed a comb from his rear pants pocket. There was just one hair out of place, and that renegade was quickly dispatched by the comb, leaving him with the image of sheer perfection.

Now that he was ready to present himself to the public, Angelo sauntered into the area where the 3rd platoon would soon be forming ranks for roll call. He glanced over at the lunch table next to the entrance to the locker room. Three white gloved TPF cops were in a huddle, obviously very concerned about the whereabouts of their fearless leader and where they were going to have roll call.

"Look at those jerks in the white gloves," Angelo laughed.

"What are you laughing at?" Joe Edwards snarled. "You should be with them on TPF like all rookies are supposed to be."

Angelo pulled his memo book holder out of his rear pants pocket and immersed himself in his opening memo book entries for the tour. He had no comeback to Joe's shot.

Angelo Petrino lived the first twenty-five years of his life as if the world was his and the rest of the population was simply present to help him with whatever he needed. Everything seemed to come easy to Angelo. To the average Joe, the blessings bestowed upon him didn't seem fair. School always came easy and right through college he was able to maintain an "A" average with a minimum effort. He also excelled at every sport he attempted, an ability that blended nicely with the athletic physique he developed when he transitioned beyond childhood. Angelo's greatest attribute was his boyish good looks. From the moment he reached puberty girls of all ages swooned over him. Being a very benevolent soul, Angelo did his best to satisfy the desires of each and every female who lusted for him, including two of his friend's mothers. With everything coming so easy to him, it was no wonder Angelo Petroni developed an attitude of entitlement. It was also no surprise when his father, Frank, a high-powered Manhattan attorney, expressed shock and disappointment at Angelo's decision to become a cop. Angelo tried to explain that he didn't want to be any run of the mill beat cop. He wanted to be a detective – one of those pinky-ring wearing, cigar chomping, designer suit wearing investigators who routinely solved the crimes of the century. Angelo's father did not want to hear about his son's crime fighting aspirations. In fact, he was determined to teach his son a lesson to make him see the error of his ways.

1983 ushered in the era of "tri-agency hiring." For the better part of the previous half century New York City had been policed by three distinct police agencies. Aside from the New York City Police

31

Department, there was also the Transit Police Department that policed the subway system, and the Housing Police Department that was responsible for the City's public housing projects. Prior to 1983, each police department conducted its own civil service exam and administered separate hiring processes. Beginning in 1983, these processes were consolidated. There was now one civil service exam for police officer with all three departments hiring from the one list. Based upon the manpower of the three departments a ratio was established for the hiring process. For every ten police officers being hired from the civil service list, seven went to the NYPD, two became transit cops, and one went to the housing police. The newly hired police officers had no say as to which department they were appointed to. On the first day of academy training, the instructors would line them up and start counting – dividing them in the proper ratio and then dropping the bombshell on some of the recruits when they were welcomed into the transit or housing police departments.

Angelo never broke a sweat when the tall thin sergeant welcomed him to the New York City Transit Police Department. In Angelo's mind, an error had obviously been made. How could he ever fulfill his destiny of becoming a famous detective as a member of the transit police. Angelo took it upon himself to leave his classroom without permission and saunter up to the administrative office on the sixth floor. There,

32

he flagged down a passing captain in the hall much as he would have addressed a college buddy.

"Excuse me, chief, you got a minute?"

The red-faced, white haired captain was stunned. "What?"

Angelo placed his hand on the captain's back. "Yeah, I'm hoping you can help me out."

The captain's eye's widened as Angelo continued. "Someone screwed up and put me in the transit police. I'm supposed to be in the NYPD, so I'm hoping you can make the change for me, buddy."

A wry smile appeared on the captain's face. "What's your name, lad?"

The captain agreed that a mistake may have been made, but not in Angelo's placement. He assisted Angelo by having him immediately driven to the Psychological Services Section of the Medical Division in Queens, to make sure no error was made in scoring his psychological test.

A second psychological test had no impact on Angelo's confidence. After that first day at the academy, Angelo hurried to the Criminal Courthouse in Queens. Angelo was not the only disappointment to his father. His sister had married a guy who had been arrested several times for a variety of crimes. On this day, his brother-in-law was standing trial in Queens for an assault that he swore he did not commit. At the time the assault allegedly occurred, Angelo had stopped by his sister's apartment and dropped off a book to his brother-in-law. This trivial act made Angelo an important alibi witness in the case. Angelo found out from cops he knew that there was usually an early release on the first day, so at 2:30 pm Angelo Petroni swaggered up to the witness stand with the confidence of a seasoned detective and provided the testimony that aided in his brother-in-law's acquittal.

Angelo figured that his stay with the transit police was temporary, but what he didn't know was that his father was determined to teach him a lesson. If his son was hell bent on rebelling against all the plans he had for him, then he was going to see to it that Angelo became the lowest form of cop. It took only a few phone calls for Frank to ensure that his son would be dumped into the depths of the transit police. He predicted that within a year his son would return to his senses and see the error of his ways.

Despite his plot, Frank was not without empathy for his son. When Angelo was about to graduate from the police academy, he explained to his father that he was going to be assigned to the Tactical Patrol Force and be required to work 8pm to 4am as a steady shift. Frank figured that his point was being made simply by his son being a transit cop, and there was no reason to inflict unreasonable torture by having him assigned to work those ungodly hours. After a few more well-placed phone calls, Angelo Petroni graduated from the police academy as the only transit police rookie not assigned to TPF.

Joe Edwards didn't try to mask his disdain for Angelo. Then again, Joe held most of his peers in contempt and he had absolutely no use for the public. The one and only joy Joe Edwards seemed to have in life was watching the reaction of people when he wrote them summonses.

The average transit cop wrote about twenty summonses a month. The younger cops who were eager to prove themselves and who hadn't yet surrendered to cynicism would tend to write a little more, but as the years wore on, summons activity lessened. Cops with over fifteen years on the job seldom wrote over ten summonses a month.

Then, there was Joe Edwards, a 22-year veteran with no wife, kids, friends, or known hobbies. The only thing this tall, barrel chested, overweight, gray haired dinosaur had was an endless supply of cutting comments for his fellow cops, and summonses for the public. Even at this advanced stage of his career, Joe was the number one summons man in District 4 by a wide margin – averaging 250 summonses a month.

It was D-Day Hoffman who anointed Joe with the nickname of "Officer McNasty," a moniker that fit his surly personality like a custom-made suit. The only member of District 4 who appreciated McNasty was Captain Morris, who could always count on inflated summons numbers because of Joe's hobby. In fact, the captain wanted to reward Joe and offered him a plainclothes anti-crime assignment or a steady partner. McNasty scoffed at the offers. All he wanted was to work alone on the 4 x 12 shift, write summonses, and make people as miserable as he was.

If not for his over the top nasty persona, Joe Edwards could easily have inherited a different nickname – ice pick. In the subway system, there were a plethora of rules and regulations, and violation of any rule could result in a summons. In reality, however, most cops wrote summonses for only a few of the regulations and those cops who wrote summonses for obscure violations were said to be ice picking people. By far, the most common rule enforced was the farebeat summons, which occurred when a violator attempted to enter the subway system without paying the fare. Also written on a regular basis were summons for violations of the Environmental Control Board which prohibited smoking and urinating in the subway system. There were some very obscure rules in the Transit Authority Rules & Regulation that no cop ever enforced – no cop except Joe "McNasty" Edwards that is.

Joe performed his own version of a stake out for summonses. A filled trash basket was the perfect location for a stake out. There was a TA rule prohibiting disturbing trash. Joe would stand on a platform near a filled basket and watch for someone who had just detrained to discard a newspaper in the basket. A perfectly good newspaper was now sitting at the top of the basket, clean and not covered with any other gook. It would not take long until someone walking along the platform spied the available newspaper and scooped it up. It was then that Joe would swoop down on his prey and write a summons for disturbing the trash. As bad as that summons was, Joe's classic ice pick summonses were written for the rule that prohibited passengers from disobeying a TA sign. Do you know how many TA signs there are in the subway system? Joe apparently did. He would stand at the bottom of any stairway and wait for an unsuspecting rider to have the audacity to begin ascending the stairs on the wrong side. He would then point to the faded paint on the wall that indicated the right side of the stairway was "up" and the left side was "down" and commence to write the summons. His best effort, however, and likely the act that would gain him admission into the summons writing hall of fame was one of his interpretations of the disobeying a TA sign rule. On the inside of all the subway car doors there were signs that read "Do not lean on the doors." Joe would stand on the platform during rush hour and wait for trains to arrive. When a particularly crowded car arrived where the occupants were packed in tighter than sardines, Joe would grab the people nearest the door when they opened and summons them for leaning on the doors.

Howard "D-Day" Hoffman, the man who was officially credited with placing the McNasty crown on Joe Edwards, was not in the muster room preparing for roll call. In fact, D-Day hadn't stood for roll call in over three months.

Cop nicknames are usually established very early in a career, or else the tag is the result of a specific incident that occurs later in a career. In D-Day's case neither circumstance applied. He had been on the job for 32-years before the nickname was thrust upon him. There had been no incident or change in his situation. The name simply revolved around a movie.

Howard Hoffman was sworn into the Transit Police Department in 1946. A little more than a year earlier, Army Ranger Hoffman burst out of a landing craft on Omaha Beach during the invasion of Normandy. Everyone knew of Howard's military experience, but in 1946 it wasn't unique, with many new cops having shared the sands of Normandy. Thirty-two years later, however, the herd had thinned with most of the veterans of the invasion of Europe having long retired. Then, in 1978, the movie Animal House was released. In the film about college fraternity hijinks there was a character named D-Day.

The movie character bore absolutely no similarities to Howard Hoffman, but that wasn't important – it was the name that mattered. So, after 32-years on the job Howard Hoffman became D-Day.

D-Day and his wife had raised six kids on Long Island, all of whom were spread out around the country with their own families. He had worked steady midnights for almost twenty years while he worked a seemingly endless amount of part time jobs to make ends meet and to get all his kids through private schools and college.

Recently, however, reality had shocked D-Day into a state of depression. D-Day was not attending roll calls anymore because three months earlier he had reached his 63rd birthday, the mandatory retirement age for police officers. D-Day just couldn't fathom spending every moment of every day of the rest of his life locked inside his home with his wife. In a desperate attempt to alter his destiny, D-Day conveniently forgot to mention to his wife that he was being forced to retire. D-Day became the biggest fan of the conventions. Five nights a week he rose from his bed at 10pm and kissed his wife goodbye at 10:30. He still traveled into Manhattan, but instead of descending into the subway and District 4 he roamed into Union Square Park and waited patiently for the convention to begin. The majority of the attendees were usually on their way by 2:30 with the hard-core partiers hanging on till around 4am. Once D-Day found himself alone he would stagger to his car and take a nap for a few hours. At 8am he was on his way home to Long Island after a long night at work, ready to hit the sack for a day of well-deserved sleep.

In the same way that McNasty Edwards was universally disliked by his peers, everyone loved D-Day, so he was always a welcomed sight at the conventions.

Ace Styles and Willie "Yes Man" Dewar shuffled their feet impatiently in the last row of rapidly assembling cops. Like race car drivers revving their engines waiting for the flag to drop, these two unlikely partners were poised for Sgt. Kelly to declare, "Fall out and take your posts!" They were assigned to Chambers Street at the World Trade Center and couldn't wait to get on post in time for the evening rush hour.

Ace and Willie were about as different as two people could be. Ace was a 38-year old rail thin white male with a long pointy nose, thin lips, pale complexion, and a receding hairline. His less than stellar appearance should not have instilled confidence, yet Ace Styles carried himself with a swagger that clearly communicated his belief that he was God's gift to women.

Willie Dewar was also 38-years of age, but this good natured, soft spoken black male seemed to have a terminal case of good humor, while Ace tended to be braggadocios and grating. Their home lives were also completely different. Ace lived in the Long Island suburbs and ostensibly was happily married for fifteen years with three teenage daughters. Willie was a lifelong resident of Brooklyn and had also been married for fifteen years. Two years ago, however, his wife passed away after a long battle with breast cancer. Maybe it was part of his grieving process, but two years after his wife's death, a single passion brought Willie and Ace together as partners - women. Their sole purpose when patrolling together was to pick up women - all women. It didn't matter the shape, size, color, ethnicity or age, all females were fair game for this dynamic duo.

Ace Styles realized his destiny at an early age. Born Joseph Blum, on his 21st birthday Ace legally changed his name to Ace Styles because he felt that Joe Blum lacked the pizazz he would need to be successful with the ladies. His marital status never deterred Ace from his passion. He rationalized that his lust for the ladies was no different than a smoker or an alcoholic. He didn't love his wife any less - it was simply an addiction he had to deal with.

As for Willie Dewar, his wife's death caused some wiring in his brain to short circuit as he rapidly transitioned from a loving caretaker spouse to a grieving husband to one of the biggest snakes on two legs. Willie's new attitude towards women was best illustrated by his nickname of "Yes Man." The moniker had nothing to do with agreement and everything to do with his name. When Willie's full name was sounded out phonetically, a question was posed - Will he do her? His answer to this question was always an unequivocal yes.

Willie looked forward to his vacation picks, and so did the rest of the 3rd platoon. For the past year and a half, during every vacation he had traveled to various locations in the world where female companionship could be purchased at reasonable prices for the duration of his stay. Last year he has visited Thailand and most recently he had returned from the Dominican Republic. Willie's return from vacation was always a big event for District 4 because he brought in his vacation pictures for everyone to see. These weren't actually pictures – they were videos. And they weren't exactly scenery shots either.

In 1984 VCRs had become commonplace, but video cameras were not yet in every household. Willie dropped a sizeable chunk of change to buy a state of the art video camera to take with him on his vacation journeys. So, what were the wonders from far-away lands that Willie recorded? His videos contained only one subject – him having sex. In the Dominican

Republic, Willie proudly stated that he found an escort service near the airport that offered one price for a different girl every day.

Captain Morris had a VCR in his office, so at the end of the shift, just before the convention, every cop from the 3rd platoon would squeeze into the Captain's office to watch Willie's vacation video. Willie could just as well have been describing the Grand Canyon, as he detailed the girl in the bed and the purpose of every thrust and gyration he was performing. Willie seemed to welcome the crowd watching him performing in his naked glory, despite the fact that he had an ample belly and wasn't particularly well endowed.

Willie continued his impatient shuffle as he looked to his right and nodded. "What's up doctor?" he greeted.

Joseph "Doctor" Dolan had joined the ranks. Ask any of the District 4 cops about the doctor and they would all say he was a nice guy. There would then be a brief hesitation before making a face and commenting that he was just something of an odd duck. Some doctor stories were famous in District 4. Many cops had experienced the doctor scream. For no apparent reason the doctor would be alone in the locker room and decide to unleash a primal scream. Everyone inside the station house would go running into the locker room to find the doctor calmly dressing at his locker.

Then there was the time the doctor was writing a farebeat summons when the subject, a huge biker type, decided to jump him. The doctor was unable to get to his radio, but thankfully, a concerned citizen ran to a pay phone and called 911. When Father Frank Mullins ran onto the scene, he observed the doctor straddling his adversary while attempting to handcuff him. The image that was burned into Frank's brain, however, was the doctor's smiling face, a huge chunk of the biker's ear clasped between his teeth. The doctor spit out the ear and calmly remarked. "I guess he didn't hear me when I asked for ID."

The doctor's bouts with erratic behavior had nothing to do with his nickname. The doctor tag was a tongue in cheek reference to his educational achievements. The doctor really was a doctor - sort of. The doctor earned a PHD from World View University - a correspondence school he found advertised on a matchbook. He was very proud of his accomplishment and claimed he did as much work as a doctorate student at NYU. He even had business cards made and began listing his name as Dr. Joseph Dolan on all his personal records and correspondence.

It was Billy Normile who eventually discovered the likely explanation for the doctor's quirky personality traits and emotional outbursts. While working together at West 4th Street on a brutally hot and humid summer evening, the doctor casually

44

mentioned that when he was nineteen years old, he had been in a plane crash. The doctor explained that he was the only passenger in single engine Cessna that developed engine trouble and crashed on a remote beach on eastern Long Island, but that he and the pilot walked away from the crash with only minor injuries. At that moment, as far as Billy Normile was concerned, the mystery had been solved. The doctor may have walked away from that aircraft with his body unscathed, but obviously, his brain had been rattled by the impact.

Father Frank Mullins joined the roll call formation next to the doctor. He gave the doctor a playful punch on the arm and smiled. "Good afternoon to you, Joe, and God bless."

The doctor stared straight ahead and mumbled the type of response that most of his comrades were accustomed to. "Good – what's good about it? At least someone thinks it's good."

No one disliked the doctor, they just found his behavior strange. Father Frank, on the other hand, actually liked the doctor. He liked talking to him and working with him. Perhaps it had something to do with his own psychosis.

Frank Mullins was always up for a good scam, and seven years earlier he struck the mother lode in scammers gold. Frank formed his own phony church in order to avoid paying taxes, and believed he was completely bulletproof as far as the IRS was concerned. Even when the government began closing in on all the fake reverends with no congregations, Frank was sure he would not be dragged down with them. Ultimately, the IRS did get around to dealing with the Reverend Frank Mullins and the Church of Universal Truth. Frank did learn an important universal truth – you don't screw with the IRS. It was only through the skill of a sharp lawyer referred to him by D-Day Hoffman that Frank was able to keep his job and stay out of jail. The lawyer may have been skilled, but he wasn't a miracle worker. Frank ended up having all his assets seized except for his house, and he had to sign a document stating that if he ever sold his house, all proceeds would be turned over to the IRS

It was universally accepted in District 4 that the ordeal with the IRS blew a couple of circuits in Frank's brain. Frank was never overly religious, even during the tenure of his sham church. Now, however, he had turned into something of a religious zealot, quoting random bible passages and greeting everyone with a warm "God bless you."

The ironic part of Frank's born-again attitude was that it was in complete contrast to his demeanor as a cop. Frank tended to be "heavy-handed," meaning that he took no disrespect from perpetrators. If Frank even perceived a verbal slight, the thumping would commence, whether it was in the district's cells or out on a station platform. Whenever Father Frank was administering this physical penance, he was always smiling and speaking very softly when he reassured his victims in between punches that God truly did love them. Father Frank's newfound faith in the church of the almighty beating at least in part explained his fondness for Doctor Dolan. Willie Dewar theorized that when Father Frank ran up on the scene of the doctor battling with the biker and saw a chunk of ear in the doctor's mouth, it must have been like the little girl having the vision of Mary at Fatima.

Ron Kelly slowly trudged behind the podium and slapped the clipboard down on the rotting wood pulpit. He glanced at the clock on the wall and then to the assemblage of police officers before him. Billy Normile slid by Kelly and made a quick comment as he passed. "Gee, I hope I can find a spot in the first row, sarge. Your roll calls are the best."

"Don't worry," Sgt. Kelly assured. "I'll make sure you're right in front of me."

Billy turned and placed his hand over his heart. "That's wonderful, sarge. I don't care what everyone else says about you, you're the best."

Many cops are blessed with a dark, sarcastic, biting sense of humor, but there was a time when Billy Normile was one of the best – the high priest or ha-ha and the prince of puns. Throughout the first seven of his ten years on the job the subway system was littered with the remains of the casualties of his pranks and jokes. Billy Normile was also a natural cop. He had instincts on patrol that could not be taught at the police academy. Billy could see a guy pacing on the subway platform and declare, "That guy has a gun," even though there was no visible sign of the firearm. When Ace styles said that Normile could smell a gun on a person, Johnny Alphabets innocently inquired as to what a gun smelled like.

Billy's attitude towards comedy and police work all changed approximately two years earlier. Thomas Lawson, the new Chief of the Transit Police Department had threatened to change transit cops into a bright orange uniform so that they would not be mistaken for real cops. All members of the transit police were outraged, but Billy Normile took enormous affront to this complete disrespect on the part of his new leader, and he took action.

Throughout the subway stations in District 4's downtown Manhattan jurisdiction, stickers started appearing in mass. These 5x7 stickers provided a straightforward message. In bold print across the top of the sticker was: CHIEF LAWSON SCREWS HIS MEN. The bottom of the sticker provided a visual image, but its message was just as clear. In a classic cut and paste operation, Chief Lawson's smiling face had been placed over the head of a leather clad male who was in the process of anally violating a male wearing only a leather mask who was kneeling on all fours.

When Lawson became aware of the stickers, he mobilized the entire Transit Police Special Investigations Unit to catch the culprit. SIU mapped out the locations of all the posted stickers and staked out the stations that were the most likely next targets. It took less than a week before Billy Normile was caught in the act at Prince Street. Lawson insisted that Billy be arrested for criminal mischief and terminated. Luckily for Normile, there was no automatic termination for a misdemeanor arrest and conviction, and the union contract guaranteed his right to a department trial before termination. Much to the consternation of Chief Lawson, Billy drew a merciful hearing officer for his trial who sentenced him to a thirty-day suspension and a year of dismissal probation. Billy should have considered himself extremely lucky to still have a career, but he didn't look at it that way. Since he returned from his suspension, he hadn't written one summons or made an arrest, and he informed anyone of any rank of his intention not to take another police action for the remaining ten years of his career. The hilarity of Billy Normile was now limited to a couple of quick remarks to the roll call sergeant.

John Szymankowszczyzna stood in the center of the first row waiting for roll call to begin. He held his nightstick in his right hand parallel to his body just as his academy instructors had told him was the proper stance at roll call. It mattered little to John that not once in his three years on the job had any sergeant actually required the roll call to stand at attention, he was going to do the right thing.

Johnny Alphabets was not just a nickname that was appropriate, it was necessary because it was rumored that even John did not know how to pronounce his last name. John was a big, strong, good natured guy who would do anything for anyone – he just wasn't academically gifted. McNasty Edwards was less subtle in claiming that John was the stupidest Polock he had ever met.

John's lack of academic prowess was almost the undoing of his career before it had a chance to begin. The academic police academy curriculum was not terribly challenging, but Johnny was not the normal student and he failed the law portion of the final exam. John was placed into the holdover program that allowed the failing recruit one additional month for the instructors to try to drill the material into their heads. After the month, another exam was administered, and if the score on this holdover exam brought the overall average up to a passing grade, the recruit was graduated and shipped out to a command. If not, the recruit was terminated.

The god that protects the stupid must have been smiling on Johnny Alphabets because he barely passed the holdover law exam with a 70. John was assigned to TPF for six months and when a new class graduated, he was able to get off TPF and into District 4. When John arrived in District 4, he was still very unsure about his knowledge of the law. Eddie McDaniel tried to put him at ease by telling him that it really didn't matter if he knew the law, because it would be clear on patrol that someone did something illegal, even if he wasn't exactly sure what the offense was. Eddie recommended to John that when this occurred, he should simply bring the offender into the station house and let the desk officer figure out what the specific offense was.

Eddie's advice may have made Johnny feel more comfortable bringing a prisoner into the command, but it didn't help his ability in filling out the arrest paperwork. To a cop with average intelligence the variety of different forms that had to be completed for each arrest could be a daunting task, for Johnny Alphabets it was near impossible. A year earlier Johnny had set the record for the longest prisoner processing time in the command – a little more than eight hours. On his record setting day, the 3rd platoon had just turned out and were filing through the district door onto the station mezzanine. Just as Johnny stepped through the door, there was a high-pitched female scream followed by the thump of Johns huge armed closing around a stunned figure.

Belinda Gomez was in the process of switching from the R train to the 4 train on her way home from work when eighteen-year old Michael Turner sprinted past her and snatched the gold chain from around her neck. The only problem for Michael was that he sprinted directly into the arms of a stunned Johnny Alphabets.

The chain snatch was a grand larceny, and a great collar for a transit cop. John was back in the district with his prisoner lodged in a cell within five minutes. That's when the fun began. Sergeant Joseph JoJo Palermo had just relieved the desk officer and would be on the desk for the entire 3rd platoon. JoJo didn't have much patience for anything, but he especially had no patience for improper arrest paperwork. When a cop was processing an arrest, the cop would fill out all the required forms and then present them to the desk officer to review and sign. Most "normal" desk officers would point out any errors to the arresting officer and tell him how to correct it. JoJo, however, was determined never to do any work for the cops. Whenever arrest paperwork was submitted for his review, if he found an error, he would simply snarl "Wrong" before tossing the package back to the cop. If the arresting officer had the temerity to question what the error was, JoJo would growl, "You figure it out!"

Johnny Alphabets never even reached the point of asking the sergeant what the error was. After the first time JoJo threw the paperwork back at him, he would go back to the arrest processing area and sit staring into space before returning to the desk with the same paperwork. Time after time he received the standard "Wrong" followed by the flying papers, and time after time John returned to the processing area praying that another cop would enter the district with an arrest so that he could get assistance. This time, however, the god of the simple was not smiling on Johnny, as the entire eight-hour shift passed without another cop entering the arrest processing area. Finally, JoJo was relieved on the desk by Lieutenant Phil Olsen, the midnight shift desk officer and a reasonable man. Lt. Olsen entered the arrest processing area and calmly asked Johnny what the problem was. After the Lieutenant pointed out where the corrections needed to be made, Johnny Alphabets and his hungry prisoner were on their way to central booking to lodge the prisoner.

Only one member of the 3rd platoon entered the muster room from a location other than the men's locker room. In 1984 female police officers were not an uncommon sight, but they certainly were common, especially in the Transit Police. When the ladies began appearing in District 4 in 1980, the commanding officer directed that a few lockers be moved into the lady's restroom so that a woman's locker room could be established. There were now five lockers in the bathroom, with Alexa "Lexi" Crosby being the only female working on the 3rd platoon.

Twenty-five-year old Lexi Crosby didn't really walk into the muster room – she swaggered. She moved with her shoulders back as if she was superior to those taking up space in her world. Lexi sauntered across the room in a sort of free-style motion that clearly communicated she was very happy with who she was. John Wayne would have been envious with the quality of her strut.

For all her bluster, there was a comedic quality to all five feet of Lexi Crosby as she sashayed along the subway mezzanine with her night stick attached to her belt almost dragging on the ground.

When Alexa Crosby arrived in District 4 in 1981, she instantly became the toast of the town. The tiny cop certainly knew how to strut her one hundred pounds in front of the drooling male population. It was easy for Lexi to cast her spell, considering her blue eyes, gold hair, and sexy strut that told the world she was beautiful.

The honeymoon between Lexi and most of District 4 was over within a year of her arrival. All the cops were falling over themselves to be nice to Lexi because each of them believed there was a remote chance they could end up in her pants, although Ace Styles and Willie Dewar were the only ones who would openly admit to that desire.

There was no formal policy regarding the females on patrol, but with a few girls sprinkled around the districts, the commanding officers unofficially took the step of always placing the female officers on a dual patrol post. This was an especially easy mission for Captain Morris in District 4 because of all the large station complexes in downtown Manhattan that were two-man posts. In the average 3rd platoon roll call, approximately half the cops worked alone while the other half worked with a partner.

The blow to the Lexi Crosby fan club occurred during the first and only time she was required to work alone. The Tactical Patrol Force had not yet been reactivated when Lexi graduated from the academy, so she was assigned directly into a rotating squad in District 4. Lexi rotated between the three platoons with four days working and two days off. During her first three months in the command, the commanding officer's unofficial mandate held true to form, and Lexi worked every tour with a partner. Then, one cold winter's night, Lexi's world was rocked. She arrived at District 4 for a midnight shift and was aghast to see that she was on the roll call to work a solo patrol post. Lexi approached Lt. McEvoy like a customer who had been given the wrong food order at a restaurant and demanded that the mistake be corrected immediately. Lt. McEvoy, a thirty-year veteran with no love for the prospect of women infiltrating his boys club told Lexi very calmly that on his tour on this night, she was going to work alone like all the other cops do. Lexi was devastated, but after roll she proceeded to her post at Broad Street in the financial district. As soon as she called on post she immediately ran to a payphone and called her boyfriend.

John Taylor had been dating Lexi ever since she graduated the police academy. As a matter of fact, their relationship began in the early stages of academy training, but that fact had to be kept very quiet since academy instructors were prohibited from fraternizing with recruits. A physical tactics instructor, who had been on the job for twelve years, John quickly fell under Lexi's spell, the sight of her prancing around the gym floor being irresistible, even if it meant jeopardizing his academy detail. The secret relationship was maintained, but now, at 12:20am Lexi had just woken her boyfriend out of a sound sleep to cry how unfair it was for her to work alone.

Lexi's magic spell was still in full force. Within five minutes after Lexi hung up the phone, John Taylor was in his car and driving from his Brooklyn apartment to Lower Manhattan. By 1am John was keeping his girlfriend company next to the Broad Street token booth. When Lexi's 3am meal period arrived, John suggested that they spend the hour in the comfort of John's car, which was parked right next to the subway stairs.

In the early 80s, the downtown financial district was dead at 3am on a weeknight, especially a cold weeknight. Doris Gladstone couldn't take Simba's barking anymore. The spoiled Maltese wanted to go for a walk and wasn't going to take no for an answer. As she always ended up doing, Doris indulged her pet's whims and within five minutes, a half-asleep woman and her very happy dog were walking along Broad Street.

Simba stopped to concentrate on a fire hydrant, but something on the next block caught the attention of Doris' half opened eyes. She tried to focus her eyes as she yanked Simba's leash to pull him closer to the building line. Was that a police officer she saw being ushered into that car – a very small female cop being put into the car by a very large black man? When the car door slammed shut, Doris crept very slowly along the building line, urging Simba to remain quiet. She got to within approximately thirty feet of the car and suddenly stopped, her eyes and mouth now wide. The streetlight provided some visibility into the car, and what she saw was shocking. She could see the back of the huge man thrusting up and down in the back seat. Oh God! Doris clamped her hand over her mouth to stifle herself from making any sounds. The female cop was being raped. Doris turned and ran away from the location of the vehicle. Simba was thrilled that his walk now included a run, but he was forced to come to a sudden stop when Doris reached the pay phone.

Two minutes later, the sirens began sounding in the distance. Very quickly the sound increased in volume and number. Finally, blue and red lights bounced off all the huge buildings as NYPD and Transit RMPs screeched to a stop on all sides of John Taylor's car.

John Taylor found himself face down on the sidewalk with revolvers sticking in both ears. A very naked Lexi Crosby tried to regain her dignity and her clothing before emerging from the back seat of the car.

In the end, no departmental charges were filed against Lexi. She was on her meal period during her back seat sexcapade, so she couldn't be written up for being off post. She probably could have been cited for being out of uniform, but the commanding officer didn't see the point.

Lexi was not going to suffer departmentally, but she certainly agonized on two other fronts. First, was the embarrassment of facing all the male cops in the district after being caught with her pants down. Most disturbing, however, was the sudden disintegration of her relationship with John Taylor. The episode had apparently been too much for her ex-boyfriend to deal with, and when he was escorted from the scene in handcuffs, he never spoke to Lexi again.

Billy Normile named the affair "The Broad at Broad Street Incident." Perhaps it was Lexi's need to re-establish her swagger that led to her demeanor on patrol. Lexi may have been short of stature, but she was large in attitude. Large in attitude as long as she had a large male partner backing her up. None of the District 4 cops had any problem backing up a partner, they just didn't like Lexi's rather big mouth that was quick to start trouble that would ultimately end up with her male partner rolling around the platform with the victim of Lexi's verbal assault while Lexi stood back and watched the melee. It was Doctor Dolan who provided an adjustment to Lexi's attitude only a week earlier.

Lexi and the doctor were near the turnstiles at the Delancey Street station when a Hispanic male called out to Lexi. The male was accompanied by his wife and two children. He tried to explain to Lexi that he had lost his wallet and that he had no money to get his family home to the Bronx. The doctor was stunned when he heard Lexi respond to the request. "I can't help you Pancho, so you better go upstairs with your family and start walking north to the Bronx – or better yet, start walking south and don't stop till you get to Mexico."

Even someone as off center as Doctor Dolan realized that the worst thing you can do is embarrass a Hispanic male in front of his family. The male was red with rage, but instead of addressing the source of the insult he turned his attention to the doctor. "You think you're tough with that badge and gun. Come over here and I'll kick your ass!"

Very uncharacteristically, the doctor maintained his composure as he walked slowly towards the irate man. "Hey, amigo. I don't want any problem with you." He slowly pointed at his partner. "But apparently, she wants to fight you, so I'll step aside and you two can go at it."

It was debatable who had the most shocked looked – the Hispanic male or Lexi. They both stared at the doctor with their mouths wide open. The doctor opened the gate and ushered the man and his family through. "Go ahead, go catch the train and get your family home."

"Thank you, sir," The man said as he ran with his family to the platform.

With the family on their way home, the doctor's supply of good nature apparently ran out. He walked up to Lexi and put his face right in front of hers. "What's wrong with you, you stupid bitch?" he screamed.

A crowd was quickly gathering as the doctor continued his verbal assault. "If you ever do that to me again, you won't have to worry about one of these assholes punching you out – I'll punch you out!" The doctor's eyes were wide with rage. "Do you understand me?" Lexi didn't answer, but the tears running down both cheeks spoke volumes.

Did the doctor's therapy session provide the needed adjustment to Lexi's attitude? Maybe. It was still too early to tell.

The only non-uniformed personnel at the roll call were Eddie McDaniel and Michael Galante, District 4's 3rd platoon anti-crime team. Eddie and Mike looked every bit the part of plainclothes New York City cops in the 1980s complete with scruffy hair and beards, and army field jackets. Captain Morris loved Eddie and Mike because they were immediately responsive to his priorities. If there was a bag snatch pattern in the district, Eddie and Mike would make a collar within a few days. If passengers were being robbed at gunpoint, before a week transpired Morris could count on his anti-crime team walking into the district holding a prisoner and a gun taken off the perpetrator.

Eddie and Mike were excellent crimefighters, but they also had many other hobbies. When there were no noteworthy crime patterns to address, Eddie and Mike could usually be found in the underground bowling alley in Greenwich Village or at the movie theatre on Canal Street in Chinatown.

Eddie McDaniel was a big man both in height and girth. Mike Galante's family owned a dry-cleaning business in the East Village where he still helped out at, even when he was working. Eddie's size and Mike's business experience resulted in the plainclothes team being tagged with the nickname of husky and starch, a play on the TV crimefighting duo Starsky and Hutch.

"Fall in!" Ron Kelly bellowed.

Johnny Alphabets was already at the position of attention as the rest of the assembled cops assumed positions with slightly less slouch.

Sgt. Kelly scanned his horizon. "Anyone seen Paddy or Legend?"

"We're coming, sarge," Paddy McGrath declared as he led Larry Holland through the locker room door and into the muster room.

"Thank you for joining us Paddy," Sgt. Kelly mocked. "I hope it's not too much of an imposition."

Paddy McGrath shook his head as he joined the roll call ranks. "Sorry, sarge, but my biological clock is way off this week."

Paddy McGrath was an eighteen-year veteran who spent his last ten years working steady midnights. The midnight shifts allowed Paddy to work full time during the day running his Long Island landscaping company. It was certainly not a love of landscaping that kept Paddy in the business, it was survival. With six kids in different stages of private grammar and high schools, Paddy needed every cent his police salary and landscaping business could garner.

An inquisitive mind might ask – wait a minute. How could this man work all day and all night? When did he sleep? The answer was quite simple. Paddy McGrath usually slept all night during his shift. He didn't just catch a quick nap in a filthy porter's room. Paddy had set up an elaborate network of subway bedrooms throughout the District 4 stations. His most essential piece of police equipment was his rope hammock that could fit into his pocket when completed folded. All he needed was access to a room with some way to mount both sides of the hammock, such as pipes or door knobs, and he was set. He even had an early warning system set up. Paddy only used rooms that had a transit phone inside. He was friendly

63

with all the token booth clerks in the District 4 area, and he would use them as lookouts. Whenever a sergeant appeared on a station where Paddy was slumbering, the clerk would call Paddy's room and he would quickly be standing tall for the arriving supervisor.

There was a fascinating dynamic that existed between Paddy and Jim Bondi. Jim was a steady midnight sergeant and seemed to have made it his mission in life to catch Paddy sleeping on the job, a goal that he had yet to attain. What made the situation bizarre was the fact that Paddy and the sergeant were neighbors in the same Long Island neighborhood that was fifty miles east of Manhattan. Although they never socialized or spoke while off duty, Paddy and Jim car pooled in an effort to save money. They would show up to work together, and then Sgt. Bondi would spend the next eight hours trying to find Paddy's hiding spot. At 8am they would get back in the same car and silently return to Long Island.

The other cops on the midnight shift referred to this odd couple as Ralph Wolf and Sam Sheepdog in honor of the 1960s animated cartoon characters. The cartoon series was built around the satiric idea that both Ralph and Sam were blue collar workers who were just doing their jobs. Most of the cartoons began at the beginning of the workday, in which they both arrived with lunch pails at a sheep-grazing meadow, exchanged pleasant chitchat, and punched into the same time clock. Work having officially begun with the morning whistle at 8:00 AM, Ralph repeatedly tried very hard to abduct the helpless sheep and invariably failed. At the end-of-the-day whistle at 5:00 PM, Ralph and Sam punched out their time- cards, again chatted amiably, and left, presumably only to come back the next day and do it all over again.

Paddy's comment to Sgt. Kelly regarding his biological clock being off was spawned by the fact that being on a 4 x 12 shift was foreign territory to him. All cops had the contractual right to work a week of their vacation to make the extra money in lieu of taking the time off. Paddy always worked his vacation and during every prior year he was kept on his familiar midnight shift for the vacation week. The contract promised no guarantees of when or where the vacation week would be served, so Paddy was shocked when he was notified that his vacation week would be performed on the 3rd platoon.

Larry Holland followed Paddy past Sgt. Kelly and into the roll call ranks. Larry was a short, slim, unassuming soul with eight years on the job. At times he was timid to the point of being painfully shy. Still, he managed to do his job, and no one had a bad word to say about him. Larry always appeared to be on the verge of exhaustion, and for good reason. Life had worn him out. Larry and his wife were the parents of a severely handicapped ten-year-old boy, and they needed his wife's full-time salary to get their son the treatment and therapy that Larry's medical benefits did not completely cover. Every day, his wife would rush home from work just in time for Larry to speed off to District 4.

Larry was forever promoted to legend status about six months earlier. Captain Morris was catching heat from headquarters about low summons activity in District 4. The captain, in turn, did what most leaders do and threatened his men. He decided to make an example of a few cops by taking them off their steady tours and putting them into rotating squads. When Larry Holland was called into the captain's office prior to the 3rd platoon roll call he had no idea why the captain wanted to see him. Maybe it was the captain's cavalier attitude, or maybe it was just the final lump of shit that caused Larry Holland's house of cards to tumble. Whatever the reason, upon hearing that his 4x12 tours were being taken from him, shy, reserved Larry Holland didn't say a word, and instead lunged across the captain's desk in an attempt to grab him by the throat. To his credit, Captain Morris was able to avoid the assault and took off running for his office door. Larry was too quick for the captain and was able to block his escape. Captain Morris ended up running in a circle around his desk with Larry Holland in close pursuit. During one of the laps the captain made a break through the door and out to the administrative area of the command. He continued running past the desk officer, through the door and out onto the mezzanine with Larry still in hot pursuit. Larry chased Captain Morris up to the street and into Union Square Park before he was finally subdued by several cops who had joined in the chase. The rescuers had arrived in the nick up time because Captain Morris had climbed a tree and Larry had just begun to climb after him when Billy Normile grabbed a hold of his leg and pulled him down.

Captain Morris did not take any official disciplinary action against Larry, most likely because he did not want to officially document the story of being chased up a tree. Instead, he sent Larry to the Employees Assistance Unit for counselling. The story had a happy ending because after hearing about Larry's home hardships, the counselor recommended that he keep his steady 4x12 tours, and as an added bonus, Larry Holland would forever be known in District 4 as *the Legend.*

Now that his cursory glance had accounted for all his troops, Ron Kelly inhaled deeply and prepared to formally call the roll.

"Styles – Dewar."

"Here sarge – here sarge."

"Chambers on the 'A' – 2000 and 2100 meals."

Before Sgt. Kelly could call out the next assignment, Sy Goldenberg popped into the muster room. "Hey Ron, don't dismiss the roll call until the captain has a word with them."

Fifty-year old Seymour Goldenberg was the black sheep of his tribe. In a family where his father was an orthopedic surgeon, his older brother a lawyer and his younger brother a pediatrician, Sy the transit cop was the relative no one dared mention at family gatherings. As disappointing as Sy was to his family, he was a godsend for Captain Morris. As District 4's administrative sergeant, Sy ran the administrative functions of the command like a finely tuned clock. With a business degree from Baruch College, running the inner workings of the district came easy to Sy – so easy that he could spend half his day lifting weights in the small district gym in the back of the locker room.

If the regular workouts were having an effect, it wasn't evident in Sy's appearance. Below his completely bald head was absolutely no muscle tone in any portion of his body. Still, Sy was extremely proud of his developing strength. Whenever he would find any young cops having meal in the muster room, he would always engage them with feats of strength like tearing a telephone book in half, a feat he had yet to successfully complete. Like any good administrator, however, he was attempting his project in sections. One day he might try to tear the book from A – E and the next time from F-L. The result was that the shelf in the muster room containing all the city's phone books contained directories that were in various stages of being ripped apart. Just a few days earlier McNasty Edwards was standing at the muster room pay phone trying to locate a particular auto body shop in Brooklyn. Suddenly, the quiet of the moment was pierced by Joe's rant. "I don't believe this," he yelled as he hurled the yellow pages across the muster room. "The pages are missing! That god damn Jewish Charles Atlas tore the pages out!"

Aside from McNasty Edwards, everyone liked Sy Goldenberg. Not only was he good natured, but he was patient and a wealth of knowledge regarding anything a cop needed to know, such as time-cards, overtime codes, and vacation picks. Sy's strong man routine was a small price to pay, even when he would constantly challenge the bigger, younger cops to arm wrestling contests. So far, all the challenged cops had let Sy win, but Eddie McDaniel was trying to arrange an arm wrestling match between Sy and Johnny Alphabets where Eddie was going to get the entire 3rd platoon to tell Johnny that the pride of the entire platoon rested on his defeat of Sy Goldenberg.

Ron Kelly continued the roll call. "Mullins – Dolan."

"Here sarge," Father Frank responded in a normal tone.

"PRESENT!" Doctor Dolan screamed at the top of his lungs.

Sgt. Kelly squinted with his mouth wide open as he glared at a very calm Joe Dolan, who was now writing in his memo book.

Billy Normile broke the silence. "It's ok, sarge. It's just gonna be a full moon tonight."

Kelly slowly returned his attention to his clipboard. "Mullins and Dolan – you have West 4th Street – 1900 and 2000 meals."

"Edwards."

McNasty responded to his name with a loud grunt.

"14th Street and 8th Avenue – 2000 meal."

Sometimes it takes months or years for a nickname to catch on, but every once in a while the stars are lined up correctly for a moniker to stick immediately. Such was the case at this roll call.

"Petroni – Crosby."

"Here sarge - Here sarge."

"Broadway-Lafayette; 2000 and 2100 meals."

Billy Normile spoke low enough to be out of range of Sgt. Kelly but loud enough to prompt a laugh from most of the assembled cops. "Looks like it's the Ken and Barbie show tonight at Broadway-Laf."

"Is there a problem?" Sgt. Kelly snarled in response to the guffaws.

Angelo Petroni took no offense to the comment. He agreed with the remark alluding to his good looks. And Lexi Crosby was not about to make any waves. She was just happy she was not working alone.

"Normile."

"Present, sarge."

"Billy, you have the home post outside"

"McGrath."

"Here, sir."

"Paddy, you have South Ferry to 28th Street on the #1 line – 2100 meal."

"Perfect," Paddy mumbled under his breath. The gleeful comment was his recognition that with his post consisting of eight stations, it would be next to impossible for a sergeant to track his whereabouts. He might just be able to stick to his normal midnight routine of getting a full shift's sleep.

Sgt. Kelly stared at the figure standing at attention directly in front of him. "Johnny," he wasn't even going to try his last name.

"Yes, sir," Johnny responded.

"You got 23rd to 33rd on the Lex line. Your meal is ....."

Before Kelly could reveal Johnny's assigned meal period, JoJo Palermo waddled into the muster room.

Joseph JoJo Palermo was without question the most hated member of District 4. McNasty Edwards was just a miserable prick, and everyone recognized that, but there was something different about JoJo. Maybe it was because he was a sergeant and had no reservations about hurting cops, even for very minor infractions of the rules. Perhaps it was also because JoJo made no attempt to abide by the same rules he would jam up cops for violating.

JoJo Palermo was the perfect foil for cops to hate and torture. He stood 6-feet tall and weighed 450 pounds – that's not a misprint – 450-pounds. His weight alone was reason enough to place a rather large target on his back, with every jokester and prankster in the command constantly trying to score a bullseye. Billy Normile, back in the days when he still cared about police work and pranks, hit perhaps the greatest bullseye on JoJo.

Even though everyone realized JoJo was over 400 pounds, he would never admit to his weight, and there was no way anyone was ever going to get him on a scale, even if a scale could accommodate his bulk. It became the impossible quest – like finding the holy grail – to get an accurate reading of JoJo's weight. One day, Billy was assigned to drive JoJo to a critical incident management seminar being conducted at the New Jersey State Police Academy. D-Day Hoffman said for the next two years that if Billy Normile would have been on Omaha Beach, they would have had half the casualties because of Billy's ability to improvise and think on his feet. What prompted D-Day's complement was the plan Billy hatched simply by acknowledging a road sign as he tooled down the New Jersey Turnpike. The sign was "Truck Weigh Station – 1 mile." Instantly, the light bulb illuminated over Billy's head.

"Sarge, I really gotta take a leak. I'm not gonna make it to the academy."

As usual, JoJo was annoyed. "What are you gonna do – piss on the side of the road?"

Billy pointed up ahead and to the right. "There's a weigh station up ahead. They have to have a bathroom."

JoJo stuck the last piece of the three chocolate donuts he had devoured into his mouth. "Just be quick about it."

Billy rolled down his window as he approached the attendant's booth. "Hey buddy, you got a men's room here?"

The attendant pointed ahead and to the right. *Score!* He would have to drive directly over the scales. As the Transit Police RMP 415, a Dodge Ram charger made it to the center of the truck scale, Billy stopped.

"What are you stopping for?" JoJo bellowed.

Billy scanned the horizon. "Where did he say that bathroom was?"

"Over there!" JoJo blurted. "To the right – are you blind?"

"Sorry sarge," Billy apologized. "I see it."

As Billy pulled off the scales his heart was racing. He had seen it alright, but it wasn't the bathroom he was referring to. He had seen the reading on the truck scale. He parked the vehicle and sprinted into the bathroom, but he did not go to the urinal. Instead he took out his wallet and removed the first useless business card he found. He grabbed his pen and wrote the weight on the scale on the back of the card – mission accomplished.

The next day Billy was scheduled to work his usual 4 x 12 shift, but he arrived at District 4 at 11am.

He went immediately to Sy Goldenberg and asked him for the paperwork and manuals on the District's vehicles. He then waited for RMP 415, the same vehicle he drove the day before, to come back to District 4 so that Sergeant Jones could take his lunch break. Once the vehicle was parked, Billy ran upstairs with a bathroom scale he brought from home and proceeded to weigh every item and piece of equipment that was in the vehicle. Once all his information had been compiled Billy retreated to an empty desk in the administrative area and began furiously typing.

No One actually saw Billy post it on the bulletin board, but as the 3rd platoon began meandering into the muster room before roll call, someone saw it. Soon, everyone was jammed around the freshly typed report.

Analysis of RMP 415

Recorded weight of vehicle –4956

weight of vehicle as per vehicle manual – 4223

weight of all items and equipment inside vehicle – 87

weight of personnel occupying vehicle – 195

unaccounted for bulk: 451 pounds

It was the perfect crime. Everyone knew what the unaccounted bulk referred to but JoJo couldn't do anything about it because his name was not mentioned.

The incident did, however, add to the hate JoJo held for the cops in District 4, in particular Billy Normile.

JoJo addressed the reason for the interruption of the roll call. "Dave Martinez just banged in with an emergency excusal. I'm gonna need a driver."

Police Officer Dave Martinez was JoJo's steady driver, not because JoJo liked him – he just hated Dave the least. JoJo scanned the assembled cops and realized as he drifted from face to face, that he hated one worse than the next. Finally, he focused in on Johnny Alphabets, still standing at attention in the center of the first row. JoJo didn't know Johnny long enough to truly hate him, so he was obviously his best choice.

"You!" He pointed a fat finger at Johnny. "Yeah, you, the kid with the long last name. You're driving me today."

Paddy McGrath poked Johnny's back and whispered. "Buy him a dozen pork rolls and he'll be your best friend."

Ron Kelly looked down the hall and saw Captain Morris making his way towards the muster room. "Ok everyone, pipe down and listen up. The captain wants to address the roll call."

Arnold Morris was clearly not the poster boy for dynamic leadership. The cops had dubbed him "Mr.

Lucky Saturday," as a testament to his leadership prowess. Promotions to sergeant. lieutenant and captain were made via civil service examinations. Further advancement to the ranks of deputy inspector, inspector, deputy chief, and assistant chief were made via appointment by the chief of the department. Since the promotional exams were always given on a Saturday, all a member of the service needed to progress to the rank of captain were good scores on three exams – in other words, three lucky Saturday's.

Some higher-ranking officers didn't know the first thing about leadership, but at least they looked the part. Arnold Morris looked as inept as he appeared to be. He was 48-years old with 21-years on the job. He was short and frail looking with thinning hair, and he walked with a noticeable hunch. Arnold used to be grossly overweight, but about five years earlier he had lost one hundred pounds. Most people look more vibrant after weight loss, but Arnold looked like he was seriously ill. Contributing to his sickly appearance were his clothes. Arnold wore suits that were at least three sizes too big because he never changed his wardrobe after his weight loss. Either Arnold was too cheap to splurge for new clothes or he assumed he would eventually gain the weight back. The result was a small defeated looking man who walked with his head down while his jacket and pants flapped in the breeze.

Captain Morris always seemed to be looking down, except when he was addressing the roll calls. He still was incapable of looking anyone in the eye, but instead of looking down, his eyes always strayed up to the ceiling while he was addressing the troops.

Captain Morris cleared his throat three times before commencing his speech. "Good afternoon men," he began, completely ignoring the fact that Lexi Crosby was at the roll call. "I just have a brief word about summons activity."

A collective groan sounded from the ranks.

"Pipe down!" Sgt. Kelly blurted.

"I know no one likes to hear it," Arnold shrugged, "but summons activity is a big part of your job."

Arnold's gaze had already shifted to the ceiling as he droned on about the importance of writing summonses. The veteran cops had already seen the ceiling stare before, and their response was always the same. One by one, much to the chagrin of Sgt. Kelly, the entire platoon began staring at the ceiling with confused looks on their faces, making it appear that they were trying to figure out what the captain was looking at on the ceiling.

Johnny Alphabets had never witnessed one of the captain's speeches before, so he had no answer when Paddy McGrath poked him in the back and leaned in to ask him what the captain was looking at on the ceiling. Paddy was just initiating Johnny Alphabets to the eccentricities of their fearless leader. No one, especially Paddy, anticipated what happened next.

Captain Morris finished his diatribe regarding the virtues of summons writing, and while still staring at the ceiling he asked if there were any questions. There was a collective shock throughout the ranks when Johnny Alphabets raised his hand and made an innocent inquiry.

"Is there anything wrong with the ceiling, captain?"

Ron Kelly dropped his clipboard, and Billy Normile almost fell backwards into the arms of Eddie McDaniel.

"What?" The captain squinted.

Before Johnny had the opportunity to repeat his inquiry, Sgt. Kelly beat him to the punch. "The color of the day is red." Ron quickly glanced at Husky and Starch who wiggled the red arm bands that were required for the day so that plainclothes officers could be identified as cops by uniformed officers at the scene of a police action.

Sgt. Kelly completed the roll call with one final command. "Ok, fall out and take your posts!"

As the snickering platoon filed out of the muster room, Arnold Morris scratched his head and turned to Ron Kelly. "What was that cop talking about with the ceiling."

"Don't worry about it boss. That cop is not very bright."

"Oh, Ok," Arnold nodded, accepting Kelly's explanation without further questions. The captain then looked down to the floor and returned to his office.

THE SHIFT

Tuesday: 4:30 pm 14th Street & 8th Avenue

Joe McNasty Edwards was already hard at work. He had been on post for no more than a half hour and had already written three summonses for smoking, disturbing the trash, and disobeying a TA sign. As he entered the details of the last summons into his memo book, he allowed himself a moment to feel good. At this rate he could easily write fifteen summonses on the shift, and maybe even twenty.

Joe's projections were momentarily cancelled by the female voice to his right.

"Excuse me, officer."

"What?" McNasty growled.

The middle-aged woman pointed down the long mezzanine toward the 16th Street end of the station. "I saw something strange down there – where that construction is taking place."

"What did you see?" Joe snarled.

"I don't know," the woman shrugged. "You better go look for yourself."

"Jesus Christ!" Joe lamented as he began the two-block underground trek across the long mezzanine.

Just before reaching the exit to 16th Street, plywood barriers had been erected to protect the construction of a new stairway to the platform. As was the norm for many transit construction projects, the work had been started, but then suddenly stopped, with no workers appearing on the site for over two weeks. The plywood structure also had a makeshift door that was not locked. In fact, it was wide open, a perfect spot for one of the many homeless residents of the subway system.

Joe approached the open door with his flashlight in his hand. As he got within about ten feet of the open door, he recognized what strange thing the lady had seen. He shined his light on a hand that was protruding out the door.

"Aw, shit," Joe grumbled. He hoped and prayed that the hand might belong to a sleeping skell – a homeless bum he could just wake up, send on his way and then return to his summons writing activities. His hope of a quick resolution quickly faded when he got closer to the door and got a whiff of that all too familiar smell. Once his light illuminated the interior of the structure, it was clear the hand was attached to a very dead body, one that had been dead for many hours, and possibly days.

Joe blurted every curse he had heard of, and some he hadn't heard of, as he grabbed the radio out of its case and brought it up to his mouth. "14th and 8th to central k."

As far as Joe was concerned, his night was ruined. He was now going to have to sit on a ripe DOA for several hours when he could be having fun harassing the public with summonses.

"14th and 8th go with your message."

"Yeah central, I'm gonna need supervision and a bus for a DOA on the station."

"What's your specific location?"

"Mezzanine at the 16th Street end of the station."

"10-4 the sergeant and an ambulance have been dispatched."

Joe Edwards never considered that the demise of the poor unfortunate soul was from anything but natural causes. He never considered protecting a potential crime scene. Instead, he took out his night stick and pushed the deceased's hand through the doorway to the interior of the enclosure. He then pulled the door closed and waited for the sergeant.

After years of bearing witness to the darker sides of life, Joe Edwards had no more sentimentality for the dead. It was easier not to think of them as people at all. Indeed, what little sense of humor McNasty possessed had become warped and darkly macabre. He opened the door again and shined his light directly on the man's face. This poor soul was someone's son and possibly a father to sons and daughters, but the only reaction Joe could muster was to snicker at the silly expression etched on the man's face. The man's race was uncertain because like most dead bodies his skin was grey tinged, with his blue lips highlighting a blank stare. Joe Edwards was irreverent about everything, so why would death be any different. Perhaps Joe was no different than any other police officer with his irreverence being a tactic to keep him sane. There was only so much horror a person could take in and understand, before the mind snapped. So, Joe Edwards joked at the unfortunate homeless man who crawled into a plywood shelter to find a place to sleep and ended up finding a final resting place.

Five minutes later the jingling of keys and equipment signaled the noisy arrival of police officers descending the 16th Street stairs. JoJo Palermo was breathing heavily even though his trip had been down the stairs.

"Hey Edwards," he bellowed while extending his arms to the side. "Where's the body?"

"Over there," Joe pointed to his left. "Inside that construction shed - a homeless skell who went to sleep in there and never woke up."

JoJo looked to his right. "Ok, whatever your name is, open the gate."

"Yes sir," Johnny Alphabets shot back.

Almost every transit lock in the system was opened with a 400 key. The average transit cop carried a key ring with approximately thirty keys on it, but the 400 key was usually the only key ever utilized.

The 16th street side of the station was not a full-time entry point. The token booth was only open during certain days and hours, but riders could still enter and exit at 16th street via steel high wheels. These devices were like revolving doors where one person at a time could push through to enter or exit. The only catch was that when the token booth was closed, a rider already had to have a token to enter. Cops and TA employees with a 400 key could simply unlock the padlock and open the steel gate to enter. Johnny Alphabets discovered the conundrum first. No matter how hard he tried, his 400 key would not open the lock. Finally, he made one attempt too many and his key snapped.

"That's just great." JoJo fumed. "Now the lock will never open."

Johnny grinned and reached into his pocket. "Don't worry, sarge. They told us in the academy to always carry a token with us just for situations like this." He held his open hand out towards JoJo. "I always keep two tokens with me."

Johnny handed JoJo a token before he inserted his token and pushed through to a waiting Joe Edwards. JoJo realized he had a couple of problems to deal with. First, he couldn't get tied up too long with this stiff. He had just placed his pork roll order before he got called for this job. If he got delayed any significant amount of time, his pork rolls would be cold and stale. His most immediate problem, however, was staring him right in his face. It was clear to JoJo that he was not going to fit through the high wheel. He was certainly not going to admit to his cops that he was too fat to enter, and he had no intention of walking back to 14th Street, coming down into the station and walking two more blocks to get to the body.

"District 4 sergeant on the air k."

JoJo grabbed his radio. "4 sergeant, go."

"District 4 sergeant, there is going to be an extended wait on your ambulance at 14th and 8th."

"10-4" JoJo put his radio back in its holder. "Just wonderful," he growled.

Joe Edwards recognized JoJo's predicament and was now going to break his balls. "Hey sarge, the body is in here. Are you coming in?"

"The bus is delayed," JoJo replied. "I'm gonna get the body bag out of the RMP."

"Why don't we just wait for the ambulance?" Joe's question traveled to an empty mezzanine. JoJo was already on his way up the stairs. Joe waved a dismissive hand. "Fat asshole." He turned to Johnny Alphabets. "Have you ever seen such a fat asshole?"

Johnny shrugged. "He is rather portly."

Joe shook his head. "Ah, what's the use."

Five minutes later JoJo was back at the steel fence. He pushed the body bag through the opening in the bars to Johnny. "Bag him and we'll bring him upstairs."

Joe Edwards raised an eyebrow. "How the hell are we gonna get him out of here, the gate won't open, remember?"

"At ease, Edwards," JoJo warned. "We'll push him through the high wheel."

"What?" Joe blurted.

"That's right," Jo Jo replied. "It's quiet at this end. We'll have him through the turnstile before anyone notices."

"This is ridiculous," Joe opined.

JoJo was becoming angry. "Look Edwards, we're certainly not going to carry the stiff to 14th street, so just shut up and follow orders."

"Yes sir," Joe grinned before turning his back to JoJo and mumbling "Asshole."

"Ok kid," Joe instructed, "bring that bag over here." Joe opened the construction enclosure door and shined his light inside.

At the site of the body, Johnny Alphabets posed a question. "Should we begin CPR?"

"CPR?" Joe gasped. "Look at that stiff – rigor mortis has set in." Joe shook his head in disgust. "You are one dumb Polock, kid."

Joe Edwards offered no assistance as Johnny bagged the unfortunate man and carried him to the high wheels. From the outside, JoJo took control of the operation. "Ok, stand him up inside and push him through. I'll catch him on this side."

Johnny did as he was instructed. He placed the body bag inside the turnstile and pushed. Then, the unthinkable happened. The turnstile made a half turn and came to a complete stop. One of the steel rods in the turnstile had warped and became jammed in the fence structure. The turnstile would not move forward or backwards. The body was trapped inside the high wheel.

JoJo was panicking as he began lashing out at Johnny. "What the hell did you do? Get out here now and get this guy out of there."

Johnny rushed through the adjacent high wheel and reached through to grab a hold of the DOA. He wrapped his hands in the body bag material and pulled with all his substantial might. The turnstile didn't budge.

JoJo was frantic. "You better get him out of there, you idiot."

JoJo's terror was rubbing off on Johnny as he continued tugging on the body bag for all he was worth. Finally, he inhaled deeply and let out a scream Doctor Dolan would have been proud of as he made one great tug on the body bag. The turnstile still never moved, but Johnny ended up falling backwards and sitting on his backside. The turnstile may not have given, but the body bag could take no more. Johnny's last great tug had spit the bag and Johnny was sitting on the ground holding the bag. Inside the stuck turnstile, the blue skinned, stiff DOA was standing there in all his deceased glory.

Joe Edwards finally found something that made him happier than writing summonses. He could barely control his laughter as he keyed the button on his radio. "14th and 8th to central."

"Go with your message 14th and 8th."

89

"14th and 8th is going to need TA ironworkers at the 16th street end of the station, and we need a rush on those ironworkers."

"What's the condition requiring the rush on ironworkers?"

Joe's voice was cracking "You're gonna have to trust me central, I need a rush on those ironworkers."

JoJo had not stopped waving his arms and berating Johnny Alphabets. His floor show was beginning to draw the interest of people on both sides of the high wheels. A middle-aged woman approached Joe Edwards and tapped him on the shoulder. "Excuse me, officer, is that poor man stuck in that turnstile?"

Joe smiled. "It certainly looks that way ma'am."

The woman shook her head. "That's terrible - how long has he been in there?"

"I'm not sure," Joe shrugged. "Why don't we ask him."

Joe escorted the lady to the turnstile and made sure to keep himself between the lady and the body.

"Hey buddy," Joe called out. "How long have you been in there?"

Joe turned and stepped to the side, giving the woman a close-up view of the bulging eyes and blue skin.

"He says he's been in there for about a month," Joe giggled.

The scream faded in the distance as the woman sprinted down the mezzanine. Joe Edwards could not remember a time that he felt happier.

Wednesday: 12:15 pm

Herby Dowdle pressed the hold button and called out the news. "Captain Morris is on line two, Chief."

Chief Hall was in no mood for preliminaries or small talk. "Ok, Morris, talk fast."

"Well, Chief, the situation is still evolving."

"Evolving my ass!" Chief Hall erupted. "I want to know what happened, and I want to know now."

Arnold Morris was already staring at his office ceiling. "Well, Chief, the good news is that I met with the commanding officer of the 13th precinct, and the NYPD is as anxious to make this go away as we are."

"Go away! Go away!" The rising level of George Hall's voice caused Herby Dowdle to instinctively cower at his desk, taking up a defensive position in preparation of the impending explosion.

"Are you actually as dumb as you look, Morris?"

Arnold Morris gulped. "I'm sorry, Chief."

"Go away?" George repeated. "I'm staring at a headline that says there was a police riot in Union Square Park last night." George began rapidly scanning his desktop, apparently forgetting that he had recently hurled the newspaper at his aid. Herby

92

recognized his boss's visual search and sprinted across the floor, holding the newspaper that he had put back together.

"Here it is, Chief." he said as he dropped the headline in front of the chief.

The moment had passed, and seeing the headline only raised George's blood pressure higher. In a repeat performance of his earlier tirade, George crushed the newspaper in his right hand and threw it directly in the face of his lackie, this time knocking Herby's glasses off. Herby was instantly crawling on the floor retrieving his glasses and the newspaper.

George Hall turned his attention back to the phone. "Look, you moron, this isn't going away. Have you forgotten that there were ten police officers who needed hospital treatment."

Arnold Morris was having trouble controlling his stutter. "I know, Chief, b-b-but..."

"B-b-but what?" George mocked. "Listen and listen good, Captain Morris. I will be at District 4 to address the 3rd platoon roll call today, and when I arrive you better have all the answers for me, understand?"

Arnold's mouth opened and close several times but no words emerged.

"DO YOU UNDERSTAND?" the chief screamed.

"Yes sir, yes sir."

The click was the only cue to let Arnold know that the chief was gone. He hung up the phone and rested his elbows on his desktop, his hands cupped over his mouth and nose. He took deep deliberate breaths as he tried to bring his heart rate down. He looked up to the ceiling and stared for the next fifteen minutes.

Tuesday 4:45 pm Chambers Street

Ace Styles and Willie Dewar knew the drill. When they were assigned to the Chambers Street station, they proceeded directly to the end of the terminal where the E train terminated. This is where the entrance to the World Trade Center concourse was located, and where the populous poured into the subway at the end of the work day. This was Ace and Willie's prime patrol location because included in this population of commuters was a plethora of beautiful woman of all ages, races and ethnicities. It was like a female smorgasbord for these two connoisseurs of the opposite sex.

Willie and Ace would proceed to their favorite vantage point, a railing that allowed them to comfortably lean and watch the passing scenery. Like experienced fishermen they would use a variety of lures and bait. Sometimes it was a smile or a corny line. Those who approached the duo with a question were in instant jeopardy of being snared.

On this day, Ace was ready to try some completely new bait. He reached into his pocket and pulled out a stack of business cards. He held the stack of rubber banded cards up in his right hand. "These are what I was telling you about, Willie. They came in the mail yesterday."

"Let's see," Willie replied.

Ace unwrapped the rubber band and pulled the first card off the stack. One side of the card looked very professional. It contained Ace's name, rank, the district phone number and the transit police logo. On the reverse side, however, was a full-length photo of Ace Styles in full police uniform. Although some might consider a full-length photo on a business card a bit strange, there was certainly nothing inappropriate about it - until a closer inspection of the photo was made. There was a huge bulge in Ace's uniform trousers in the crotch area.

"What do you think?" Ace asked his partner.

"Nice," Willie nodded. "How did you get that effect?"

"I stuck six socks down my pants. Do you think it's a little overstated?"

"No, no," Willie assured his partner. "It's very subtle. I like it."

"Excuse me officers." The fishermen had been caught off guard. As they fawned over the benefits of Ace's bulging pants, two fish had swum right up to them.

Ace was immediately smitten by the girl in front of him. She looked to be in her late twenties and her tall frame and slender body were like a Victoria's Secret model. Her blue eyes, like the sea, were calm and emotionless and her long, wavy blonde hair, so smooth and silky, looked as if it was tailored from gold fabric.

Willie was focused on the other female. She may have been over forty, but in Willie's opinion she outshone her friend. She had the sort of face people forgot even before they'd stopped looking at it. She had probably gained thirty pounds since she turned forty, most likely around the hips. Still, Willie loved what he was looking at.

Ace turned on his debonair voice. "Good afternoon, what can we do for you beautiful ladies?"

They both looked at each other and giggled. "We're going to a retirement party for our co-worker, and we're not really sure how to get there."

"Where is the party?" Willie inquired.

The older lady jumped in. "Angelino's on west 16th Street."

"That's easy," Willie replied. "That's right near Union Square." He pointed to the E train sitting in the terminal. "Take the E train to 14th Street then transfer to the L and take it two stops to Union Square. Angelino's is a half block away."

The two girls smiled. "Thank you very much," the younger one said.

"It's our pleasure, girls," Ace said as he reached into his pocket.

"Here," he extended two business cards to the ladies. "That's my card. Look, when you leave your party tonight, you'll be going back to Union Square for the train. My partner and I will be attending our own party in the park. We would love for you ladies to join us."

The girls stared at the business cards and their eyes grew progressively wider as they noticed the focal point on the picture side. "I don't know," the younger girl remarked. "What time is your party?"

"We'll be there at midnight," Ace shot back.

"That's kinda late to be roaming around a park looking for you guys," the older lady remarked.

Ace held up his hands. "Look ladies. Enjoy your party, and when you get back to Union Square, if it's past midnight, stop in the park and say hello, Ok."

The two ladies looked at each other and giggled again. "ok, we'll see, the younger woman nodded."

"See you later," Ace waved as they ladies disappeared into the E train.

"What do you think?" Willie asked.

"I think it's perfect," Ace replied.

"What do you mean?"

"I mean that we were going to the convention in the park anyway tonight. That party they are going to is going to do our work for us."

"How?"

"Come on Willie, you know what I mean. When they come staggering into that park they will already be liquored up and horny. They may just take advantage of us."

Willie nodded. "That would be a real shame if that older one took advantage of me."

Ace nodded. "I think they'll be there, especially since they have my cards." He turned to Willie, "Do you think they liked the cards."

"Absolutely," Willie assured. "Like I said before, it's very subtle."

Tuesday: 5:20 pm West 4th Street

Jason Thomas was having a bad day. The 35-year old had spent the day trying to squeeze out a living by selling refrigerators and washing machines to obnoxious, ignorant, unappreciative customers. He had spent the last twelve years in the same Greenwich Village store dealing with the same ungrateful, cheap clientele. He didn't sell one appliance this day, and to add the cherry to his cake, just before the end of his shift his boss called him into his office and warned him that if his sales didn't improve, he could lose his job.

Venting constructively is an important key to keeping feelings of anger from becoming significant problems. Feelings of anger can lead to impulsive responses or ultimatums that often lead us to feelings of regret, guilt, and shame. Therefore, it is healthy for a person to blow off steam now and then. Jason's problem was that he picked the wrong place and the wrong person to blow his steam at.

The West 4th Street subway station ran under 6th Avenue between West 3rd Street and 8th Street in Greenwich Village. Billy Normile once philosophized that the station was a testimonial to the intelligence of New York City Transit management, even in the early years of the subway system. Billy gleefully pointed out the fact that the West 4th Street station had no entrance at West 4th Street.

Father Frank Mullins and Doctor Dolan leaned leisurely on the railing next to the turnstiles near token booth N80, the 8th Street side of the station. They both were lost in their thoughts as the public clicked through the turnstiles, beginning their journey's home.

Janice Clark cleared her throat in an attempt to get the attention of the daydreaming cops. The middle-aged tourist from Wyoming held a subway map open as she approached. "Excuse me officers. Can you tell me how to get to Shea Stadium in Queens?"

Doctor Dolan continued leaning on the railing, but turned his head slightly to address Janice. "Go down to the lower level and take the D train to 161st Street."

"Thank you," Janice sang as she folder her map and started down the stairs.

Jason Thomas pushed through the turnstile and identified his opportunity to blow off steam. "You just gave that woman the wrong directions," he blurted.

"What?" the doctor frowned.

Jason stood with his hands on his hips. "You heard me. You gave that woman wrong directions."

"What are you talking about?" the doctor shot back. "I told her to go to 161st Street – Yankee Stadium is right there."

"She asked for directions to Shea Stadium," Jason scoffed. "She wanted to go to Queens and you sent her to the Bronx."

The doctor continued leaning on the railing. "She'll figure it out."

Jason shook his head as he took a step toward the stairs. "Moron!"

The doctor sprung to attention. "What did you say?"

Jason made an about face and entered full steam blowing mode. "You heard me right, you moron."

Doctor Dolan squinted. "Moron?"

Father Frank smiled and shook his head. "Oh boy, here we go."

Jason continued advancing. "This is what I pay taxes for? – so incompetent boobs like you can give the public wrong information."

Father Frank remained in his leaning position and shook his head again. "I wish you hadn't said that mister."

The doctor slowly advanced towards Jason. He looked up to the ceiling and put on his best James Cagney voice. "Incompetent, the man says. How do you like that ma?"

Jason's mouth opened but no words came out. The doctor's words confused him. Before he could figure out their meaning, the doctor rushed forward and grabbed Jason around the waist. He quickly lifted the shocked salesman and deposited him in the trash basket next to the token booth. The look of shock was still planted on Jason's face as he wiggled and twisted in unsuccessful attempts to get out of the basket.

A tall man in a suit had entered through the turnstiles, but had delayed to watch the action. "That was the most outrageous thing I ever saw," the man exclaimed.

"Hey," Father Frank called from the railing. When the man acknowledged him, Frank pointed to the other side of the mezzanine. "There's another trash can over there, so if I were you I would keep walking."

One look at the doctor's eyes and the man was gone. Father Frank meandered over to the occupied trash can and gently lifted its shocked occupant out. He dusted Jason off and patted him on the back. "Have a good night sir and remember that God loves you."

Tuesday: 5:50 pm   Wall Street

Larry The Legend Holland was a man on a
mission. Even though his pursuit up a tree of Captain
Morris had ultimately resulted in him keeping his
precious 4x12 tours, he didn't want to tempt fate. He
was determined to keep his summons activity up so
that the captain would never have an excuse to revisit
the issue. Larry became like a fisherman. Whenever
he was at a location where the fish were plentiful and
biting, he pulled as many as possible out of the water.
Such was the case for his assignment to Chambers and
Wall Street, specifically Wall Street on the #2 line.
More specifically, the booth at the back end of the
station with the array of turnstiles in the shape of a
horseshoe. During the afternoon rush hour, the fish
were always biting at that location, so Larry could
satisfy his monthly summons quota with only a few
assignments to the station each month.

Larry detrained at Wall Street and went right to
work. He ascended to the mezzanine by the horseshoe
turnstile arrangement and unlocked a porter's room
adjacent to the token booth. This was a dark, filthy
room, but the Legend didn't care. The door to the
room had a small peep hole in it that served as a
perfect observation point for the turnstiles. The only
problem with the setup was that the observation post
was outside the turnstiles and the farebeat would be
inside the turnstiles when Larry popped out of the

room. As soon as he emerged from his hiding place, Larry would yell in an authoritative voice "Hey you, come back here!"

Sometimes, the farebeat obeyed and came back thru the turnstiles to Larry, but other times they didn't. In these non-compliance cases, Larry would initiate what he referred to as the "two-step pursuit." When it became clear that the farebeat was about to bolt down the stairs, Larry would pursue - for two steps. He realized that there was a near zero chance that he would catch one of these fleeing gazelles, so he saw no point to a real foot pursuit. Besides, this fishing hole was so well stocked that he could still write as many summonses as he wanted, even if some did run away.

Larry did try to abide by the rules and regulation of summons writing, the most basic of which was that a violator had to be properly identified in order to be qualified for a summons. If a person did not have ID and could not verify his identity, an arrest had to be made. Larry wasn't interested in making farebeat arrests, so he was usually fairly liberal with his identity verification process. Recently, however, Captain Morris had been cracking down on questionable summonses.

Questionable summonses came in different varieties. Some cops wrote bogus summonses. They would just make up a name and the personal information - throw out the defendant's pink copy of the summons and turn the rest in to the desk officer at the end of the tour. Paddy McGrath had actually developed something of a science to writing bogus summonses. Paddy would scan the newspapers for the lists of unclaimed funds that would appear now and then as legal notices. Paddy loved these lists because they contained names and addresses. Mike Galante once asked Paddy if he was worried about his scheme coming back to haunt him when these unclaimed funds people started complaining when they found out they had warrants for failing to appear on their summons return dates. Paddy scoffed at Mike's concern noting that if these people weren't concerned about claiming their money, they certainly weren't going to be concerned about receiving a summons.

The other variety of questionable summons was the non-identified defendant. Captain Morris had recently tasked Sy Goldenberg with performing an analysis of district 4's farebeat summonses for a six-month period, and the administrative sergeant made quick work of the assignment. Captain Morris was shocked to find that 72% of the summonses were written to defendant's who lived at 8 East 3rd Street. This address was the location of a large men's homeless shelter in Lower Manhattan. When a cop encountered a farebeat who could not properly identify himself and claimed to be homeless, the benevolent cop instantly found a home for the poor soul - at least for the purpose of the summons - at 8 East 3rd Street.

Now that the captain was on to the 8 East 3rd street scam, a bit more discretion had to be used in summons writing. Larry had his own technique for verifying identification. If the person had no ID on him and claimed that he could not provide a phone number of someone who could verify his identity, Larry would snap the handcuffs on. Larry had no intention of actually making an arrest, but it was amazing how quickly the cuffs would jar a memory, with a phone number almost immediately flowing out of the violator's mouth.

During this rush hour, the fish were virtually jumping out of the lake. Even with three runners who Larry let go after his two-step pursuit, he had already written eleven summonses. In another thirty minutes he may be able to almost fill his quota for the month.

The large envelope under his arm indicated this tall, lanky, young black male was a messenger. Messengers were like trout in a lake - they were always biting. Most messenger services supplied their messengers with a weekly stipend to cover the subway fare for the week. If a messenger could avoid paying the fare, it was like a bonus in their paycheck.

The messenger vaulted the turnstile with ease. Larry popped out of his room. "Hey, you, come back here."

This male probably could have walked faster than Larry could run, but surprisingly, he stopped, turned around and came back through the turnstiles.

Larry pointed to the wall next to the token booth. "Stand over there."

Larry performed the proper tactical maneuver of blading his body toward the male to protect his gun side in case of an attack. He removed his memo book holder from his rear pants pocket and removed a universal summons.

"Let me see some ID," he directed.

The male shrugged. "I don't have any ID."

Larry raised an eyebrow. "You're a messenger and you don't have any ID - not even a company ID."

"No."

"What company do you work for?"

"Rapid messenger on William Street."

"Well, I'll just call them to verify your identity."

The male's voice assumed a sense of urgency. "Please officer, don't call my job. I'll be fired if they find out I beat the fare."

Larry shrugged. "Well, I need a phone number of someone who can verify you."

The male shook his head. "I don't know anyone."

"Face the wall and put your hands behind you head." Larry reached to the back of his gun belt and removed his handcuffs. Two fast clicks and Larry turned the male back to face him. "Now," he continued. "You get one chance to provide me a phone number before I get on my radio and call for a car to transport an arrest - an arrest where you will spend the night in jail because you have no ID."

"718 234-5834," the male blurted. "My aunt will verify who I am."

Larry shook his head. "It's amazing how a person's memory improves with the cuffs on." He opened his memo book to expose one of the blank back pages and pulled his pen out of its holder on his belt. "Ok, young man, what's your name?"

"Ron North."

"And your address?"

Five minutes later Larry kept one eye on his cuffed prisoner while he finished up his conversation on the payphone at the bottom of the street stairway. "Thanks for your help ma'am. Yes, he'll be released in a couple of minutes. Yes, I agree, he seems like a good kid. Have a good night ma'am."

Larry hung up the phone and approached the male. He put the finishing touches on the summons before tearing out the defendant's pink copy. He held the pink paper up in front of the male and gave the same speech he had given about a thousand times before: "You are being issued a summons for theft of service. You are required to appear at Manhattan Criminal Court at 100 Centre Street on the return date listed on the summons. If you fail to appear on that date a warrant will be issued for your arrest."

Larry folded the paper neatly four times and pushed it into the male's shirt pocket.

"Ok," Larry remarked as he reached for his key ring. "Let's get you out of here."

Larry fumbled through his keys several times before looking up at the male with a blank stare on his face. "Oh, shit!"

"What's wrong?" the male asked.

"My handcuff key." Larry replied.

"What about your handcuff key?"

"It's gone!" Larry gasped.

"How are you gonna get these things off me?" the male wailed.

Larry scratched his head. "I don't know."

"You don't know?" the male whined. "I still have a delivery to make. Now I will be fired."

Larry held up his right hand. "Calm down - no one's getting fired."

Larry's problem-solving abilities had hit a stone wall. What was he going to do? He did not want to get anointed a legend for a second time, but he knew that is exactly what would happen if he had to call for Sgt. Palermo to respond to his location with a handcuff key. There was also the reality of his location – Wall Street. There were no locksmiths of hardware stores in the area. As he pondered his predicament he watched the stream of commuters push through the turnstiles. He focused on one particular man who stood out from the rest of the Wall Street crowd. The mercury had topped 90 and was likely ten degrees higher in the subway oven. In these conditions, most New Yorkers start to wilt. Many resort to shorts and tank tops. Even in the financial district more than a few stockbrokers, bankers and lawyers reached for their seersuckers. Yet amid all the casual summer wear, here was this Hasidic Jewish man wearing a dark three-piece suit crowned by a black hat made of rabbit fur. To those New Yorkers trying to beat the heat he looked painfully overdressed. To Larry Holland, however, he represented salvation.

"Abe!" Larry blurted.

"What?" Ron North asked.

"Abe the shoemaker." Larry clarified.

"I don't need no shoes," Ron scoffed.

Larry grabbed Ron by his right arm and led him through the exit gate. "Don't worry about it – just come with me."

"Where are we going?"

"You'll see," Larry grinned.

Larry led his handcuffed prisoner down to the island platform and waited for an uptown train. The platform was crowded, but the horde of New Yorkers paid absolutely no mind to the unformed cop holding tightly on to a handcuffed prisoner.

One short stop later Larry pushed Ron out to the Fulton Street platform. Fulton Street was part of the large Broadway-Nassau complex. The main Broadway-Nassau entrance was Larry's destination. At this location, there was a small mall located between the street and the station mezzanine. This mall contained four stores – a barber shop, a video game arcade, a florist, and a shoemaker.

Larry led Ron up the stairs and stopped in front of the florist, "That's where we are going." he said pointing to the sign that read ABE THE SHOEMAKER.

74-year old Abe Stein loved talking to the cops and the cops loved talking to Abe. Abe had a story for everything. He had done it all and seen it all. Abe claimed to have been imprisoned in a Nazi concentration camp during World War II, and had escaped after killing five guards with his bare hands. He said that after the war he emigrated to Israel and worked for Mossad, Israel's intelligence agency. At one time or another, Abe had claimed to be the fastest runner, the strongest swimmer, and even the most satisfying lover. He would regularly challenge the cops to arm wrestling matches, although no one had ever taken him up on the challenge.

Billy Normile was the first cop to Call Abe Commander McJew as a tribute to Commander McBragg. Commander McBragg was a cartoon character who appeared in short segments in the 1960s and 70s. The segments opened with an image of a revolving globe and the title "The World of Commander McBragg." The Commander, a retired British naval officer, would buttonhole a hapless member of his gentleman's club, and relate some story filled with unlikelihood's and outright impossibilities, always concluding with a hairbreadth escape.

Larry cared little about Abe's boasts of super strength and endurance. He focused on one claim Abe had made. Several month earlier Larry was passing through the mall when Abe caught his ear. On this occasion, Abe claimed to be the world's greatest locksmith. He had pointed to Larry's handcuff case and claimed that he could open any handcuffs in less than thirty seconds. As with the arm wrestling brag, Larry did not take him up on the handcuff challenge, but now, he had no other choice.

Ten minutes later Larry stood watch as Abe unfolded an old worn tri-fold leather case that contained over a dozen picks, pins, and hooks. Abe rubbed his fingertips with his thumbs like a safe cracker. "I haven't used these lock picks in a long time," he gulped.

Larry became anxious. "But you can open them, right?"

"Yeah, yeah." Abe unconvincingly exclaimed. "I'll open them."

Abe put on glasses equipped with a light and selected a pick from his case. "Back the young man up against the table so I can get a good look at the handcuffs."

Larry gently backed Ron into the table. "Jesus Christ, Abe, you look more like a jeweler than a locksmith."

Abe inserted the pick into the lock and began rotating the device. "Do not disturb me, and mentioning Jesus Christ is certainly not going to help the situation."

Thirty minutes later Larry had transitioned from anxiety to panic. Sweat poured down Ron's forehead but he could not wipe his brow. His hands were still securely cuffed behind his back.

Abe pushed his chair back from the table and turned off the light on his glasses. "I don't understand it," he lamented. "I've opened a thousand handcuffs – I just don't understand."

Larry was visibly shaking. "Well, I understand. You're nothing but a lying prick. Every story you've ever told is total bullshit."

Abe didn't react to Larry's verbal barrage. He slowly rose from his chair and walked to his cash register. He opened the drawer below the counter and reached inside. He returned to the table and reached across to Ron's cuffed hands. There was the unmistakable clicking sound of handcuffs opening. "There you go, young man." Abe said as he opened the second cuff.

Ron rotated his arms again and again to get the blood circulating. Abe placed the handcuffs on the table. "There you go Larry."

Larry's mouth hung wide open. "You had a key?"

"Of course, I had a key," Abe replied.

Larry extended his arms to the side with his palms up. "If you had a key, why didn't you use it."

Abe shrugged. "That would have been no fun."

Larry shuffled his feet and looked at the floor. "Abe – I'm sorry about those things I said. I was just panicking over the situation. I didn't really mean it."

Abe wave his hand at Larry. "Forget it." He looked at Ron, who was still rotating his arms. "How do your arms feel?"

Ron smiled and nodded. "They feel pretty good."

"Good," Abe said as he sat at the table. He placed his right elbow on the table and extended his hand upward. "Let's have a go at it."

"What?" Ron was confused.

"Arm wrestling" Abe clarified. "Let's do it."

Ron needed no further convincing. He pulled up a chair opposite Abe. A few seconds later there was a loud thump from hands crashing on the table followed by Abe's pained cry. "Oyeeeeeee!" Apparently, his arm wrestling skills were as rusty as his lock picking abilities.

As Larry ushered Ron out to the mall, he turned to bid farewell to the moaning shoemaker. "Thanks a lot Abe. You're a life saver."

Abe said nothing. He held his right wrist and continued to moan.

Larry walked Ron down to the token booth and let him enter through the gate. He pointed to Ron's shirt pocket. "You've been through enough today. Give me that summons back."

Ron pulled the pink paper from his pocket and handed it to Larry. Larry waved the summons in front of Ron's face. "Next time, pay your fare."

Ron smiled. "You don't have to worry about that." He gave a slight wave and a nod as he broke into a trot to catch the incoming #4 train. Larry ascended to the street and made the slow walk back to his post at Wall Street. The situation was resolved, but he still had a problem. It was very noble of him to take the summons back from Ron, but he still had to account for it. Each summons had a serial number so he couldn't just tear it up and throw it away. He would have to turn the summons in at some point.

When he returned to the Wall Street station he proceeded immediately to the semi-hygienic porter's room and locked the door behind him. He sat on an overturned bucket and placed Ron's summons on the cheap folding table. Larry was about to utilize one of the top skills of a transit cop – the ability to change letters and numbers. This skill was usually reserved for altering times of memo book entries. Written entries could not be crossed out, so if a cop needed to change a time to extend a personal break or to place himself away from the location of a reported crime, it was easy enough to change a one to a nine or a three to an eight. The same alterations could be made to several letters, and now Larry leaned over the table and studied the summons. He looked at the first name and nodded. This one was easy. All he had to do was change the "o" to an "a" and add "dy" and instantly the first name was changed from Ron to Randy. Larry stroked his chin and smiled. The last name would be just as easy. A few lines and curves later Larry looked proudly at a summons that was no longer issued to Ron North. This summons belonged to Randy Martin, with a completely different address and date of birth. Larry tucked his memo book holder back in his rear pocket. *All's well that ends well,* he thought, unless of course there was someone named Randy Martin who lived at that new address in the Bronx.

Tuesday: 6:25 pm   Broadway - Lafayette

Broadway - Lafayette was a station in the NoHo, or north of Houston Street district of Manhattan. The complex comprised two stations, Bleecker Street, on the IRT line, and Broadway - Lafayette on the IND line.

The NYC subway system had always been synonymous with words like dirty, filthy, and grimy, but the Broadway - Lafayette station represented the dirtiest, filthiest, and grimiest conditions in the city. This unenviable reputation had developed, at least in part, due to the propensity of homeless frequenting the station. In 1984 the Transit Authority had initiated Operation Enforcement, an initiative to kick the homeless out of the subway system. Unlike an earlier campaign to remove graffiti, Operation Enforcement met with considerable opposition. Advocates for the homeless and many politicians questioned the authority's intentions and tactics, calling the agency insensitive to the thousands of homeless people who lived in stations and tunnels.

Angelo Petroni and Lexi Crosby agreed with the opposition forces, not because of any empathy for the plight of the homeless, but because Ken and Barbie did not want to spoil their perfect appearances by having to handle these filthy unfortunates. The thought of having his custom-tailored shirt wrinkled interacting with one of these skells disgusted Angelo, and Lexi would freak out if she broke a nail waking up a sleeping bum.

This was the first time Angelo and Lexi had worked together, but they instinctively migrated to the Bleecker Street side of the complex because it was a physically cleaner location. They spent the first two hours of the shift ostensibly looking for farebeat summonses, but in reality, they lounged near the token booth making fun of the odd-looking people who passed them and complementing themselves and their flawless looks. Ken and Barbie were made to be partners.

In the middle of Angelo explaining his workout routine to Lexi, an elderly woman using a cane for support shuffled past them. The woman stopped and smiled at the two cops. The ever-chivalrous Angelo, interrupted the explanation of his bicep routine and tipped his cap. "Good afternoon, ma'am."

The woman nodded. "My God. I have never seen such good-looking people. Can you imagine how beautiful the children you produced would be?"

With that declaration, the woman shuffled on her way. Lexi was still blushing from the complement, but Angelo just shrugged. "She's right you know. If we had kids they'd be absolutely gorgeous."

Lexi chuckled uncomfortably. "Don't get any ideas, Angelo. Our partnership is limited to this station."

"Ok," Angelo laughed. "We'll stay on the station. We can go into the porter's room and do it there."

Before Lexi had a chance to accept his offer or threaten to report his grossly inappropriate statement, Angelo continued. "I'm just kidding Lexi."

"I know," Lexi replied.

Still, Angelo couldn't seem to leave well enough alone. "Besides, that porter's room is filthy. Are you going to the convention tonight?"

"Maybe," Lexi shrugged.

"Well, maybe we can disappear in the trees in the middle of Union Square Park," Angelo suggested. "It's a lot more sanitary there."

Lexi smiled. "I guess we'll have to see, won't we?"

Tuesday: 7:10 pm - 9th Street & Broadway

Eddie McDaniel and Mike Galante were out the district door as soon as Ron Kelly gave the order to fallout. Along with participating in the comedy of joining Captain Morris in staring at the ceiling, Husky and Starch heard the captain's message regarding the importance of summons activity. The 3rd platoon anti-crime team wanted to stay in plainclothes, so they hit the road to write summonses immediately, especially since they had plans for later in the tour that had nothing to do with police work.

Eddie and Mike descended directly to the uptown BMT platform and jumped on an R train one stop to 23rd Street. The rush hour farebeat action was good, and by 5:30pm both plainclothes cops had written ten summonses each.

With a full shift's work completed in an hour and a half, it was time to move on to the more important issues of the evening. Husky and Starch jumped on the downtown R train to 8th Street. They went immediately upstairs to Broadway and walked north a block to 9th Street. A non-descript door led to a dark stairway. In the basement a second door opened to the bright, loud world of Bowl-a-mania.

Eddie waved to the round man behind the desk. "What's up Gino?"

"Big crowd tonight," The man responded. "But I saved you boys a lane."

"Thanks, brother," Mike nodded.

"Here you go." The man placed two pair of bowling shoes on the counter. "Sizes eleven and ten, right?"

"You got it," Eddie confirmed as he and Mike grabbed the footwear."

The man nodded towards a door to his left. "Your balls are in the back room. You can go get them."

"Thanks Gino. What lane are we on?"

"You guys are on 28."

Mike Galante was breathing heavily. It wasn't the exertion of bowling that had his chest heaving, it was the excitement of anticipation. Mike squeezed the rosin bag and inserted three fingers into his ball. He took several deep breaths as he studied the distant pins. Mike was about to roll his 9th frame, with his previous eight reaping identical results – strikes. Mike was a good bowler – one of the best on the transit police team, but he had never come close to bowling a perfect game.

Mike went into his crouch and started forward. His right arm came back and he released the ball with his left foot just short of the foul line. The pins sounded like a clap of thunder – another strike.

Mike rubbed his forehead as he returned to the scorer's table. "I don't know how much longer I can take this."

Eddie McDaniel stood up and reached for his ball. "Don't be so dramatic. I once bowled a 301."

Mike sat at the table and waved his hand dismissively. "You're full of shit. A perfect game is 300."

"That's right," Eddie admitted as he approached the line. "I certainly didn't bowl a 300 and lose."

"Asshole," Mike mumbled as he scanned the nine x's in each of his nine completed frames.

Before Eddie could advance for his turn, his concentration was broken by loud static emanating from the scorer's table.

"Units in the vicinity of 8th Street on the R – signal 10-13 from the officer."

Eddie and Mike grabbed the paper bags camouflaging their police radios and dashed for the exit. As they ran past the front desk Eddie blurted. "We'll be back, Gino."

A signal 10-13 was the radio code for a police officer needing assistance. All 10-13's were taken seriously, but many of these emergency calls turned out to be unfounded, the result of pranksters making false 911 calls just to see the police responding from all directions. When the radio dispatcher noted that the call was coming from the officer, that information added an additional sense of urgency because responding officers knew the call originated from a cop.

Husky and Starch sprinted down Broadway and down into the 8th Street station. The large number of subway riders rapidly moving away from the south end of the downtown platform was a clear indicator they were running in the right direction. As they weaved through the humanity the commotion at the end of the platform came into focus. One of Certs white glove squad was patrolling a southbound R train when he took a Hispanic male off the train to write him a summons for smoking on the train. Once on the platform, the smoker apparently had a change of heart about receiving the summons and the fight was on. The cop was holding his own, but the arrival of Husky and Starch brought the struggle to an abrupt end.

Mike Galante put a "no further" over the radio, communicating that no other cops were needed at the scene. That transmission didn't stop the four NYPD officers from sprinting down the platform, nor did it deter Billy Normile from responding from 14th Street on an R train. The final cop to run onto the scene was Johnny Alphabets, which meant that JoJo Palermo would come waddling down the platform about five minutes later.

The smoker was cuffed and sitting on a bench while the TPF cop made memo book entries regarding the incident. Billy Normile exchanged pleasantries with the NYPD cops, Eddie, and Mike before settling in on the platform next to Johnny Alphabets. Billy's cynical attitude had taken him out of the prank business, but every now and then he had a relapse. Billy took a long look at Eddie and Mike, and then leaned into Johnny Alphabets.

"They're not wearing the color of the day."

"What?"

"McDaniel and Galante," Billy clarified. "They're not wearing the color of the day arm bands."

"You're right," Johnny replied. "I wonder why."

"I know why," Billy pointed to their feet. " They don't need to have the armbands because they're wearing their anti-crime shoes."

"Anti-crime shoes?" Johnny questioned.

"Sure," Billy continued pointing at the bowling shoes. "They are red and white, and look at the numbers on the back of the heels. That's their anti-crime identification numbers."

Johnny squinted as he stared at the back of the shoes while Billy continued his explanation. "McDaniel is anti-crime 11 and Galante is anti-crime 10."

Johnny nodded. "Oh yeah. I see."

Billy thought he felt the vibration of a distant train, but it was actually JoJo Palermo waddling down the platform. JoJo was usually in a foul mood, but tonight he was beside himself, just having spent a couple of hours with the homeless stiff stuck in the high wheel and missing out on his pork roll dinner. Now, before he could think about finding something else to eat he had to respond to handle the TPF cop and his resisting smoker.

The huffing and puffing rotund sergeant pointed a finger at Johnny. "Write me a list of everyone at the scene while I go deal with this bullshit."

Johnny pulled out his memo book and began scanning the NYPD cops nametags and badge numbers. Billy looked over Johnny's shoulder. "don't write their names."

"What?"

"McDaniel and Galante – don't write their names while they are in plainclothes – use their anti-crime numbers."

"Oh, Ok." Johnny put a line through the names and wrote 11 and 10 instead."

The TPF cop held firmly to his cuffed prisoner's arm as he began walking him down the platform and up to the street. Johnny Alphabets handed over his list of personnel on the scene to JoJo, an act witnessed by Billy Normile.

As Billy observed the obese sergeant looking over the list of names like a restaurant menu, he walked over to Husky and Starch. "You guys should get out of here, now."

"What's wrong?" Mike asked.

Billy looked over at JoJo and shook his head. "Trust me." He pointed to the two pair of bowling shoes. "You need to get out of here now."

JoJo had just noticed the numbers on his list. "What are these numbers – 10 and 11?"

Johnny Alphabets responded confidently. "I didn't want to list the names of plainclothes personnel, so I used their numbers."

"What?"

"I used their anti-crime numbers," Johnny clarified.

"What the hell is an anti-crime number?" JoJo bellowed.

"The numbers on their anti-crime shoes." Johnny replied.

"Anti-crime shoes?" JoJo sneered. "Are you drunk, kid?"

"Absolutely not, Sergeant Palermo. Let me explain."

JoJo shook his head. "I don't think I want to hear your explanation. Just get behind the wheel and let's drop this mope back at the district. If I'm lucky I might still be able to find a place with fresh pork rolls.

Tuesday 9:45 pm   14ᵗʰ Street / Union Square

Certs Eckhart found that he liked the 4 x 12 hours much better than the 8pm x 4am shifts, but this preference had nothing to do with his personal life. There was much more activity in the subway system at 9pm than there was at 2am, and Certs loved having a larger audience when he assembled his white glove squad for a TOMS operation. On this evening Certs had selected the downtown Lexington Avenue platform at 14th Street Union Square for his band of marauders. Certs liked this station because he could perform a more impressive drill. The location had island platforms, so on the downtown platform, the express 4 and5 trains arrived on one side of the platform while the 6 local utilized the other side of the platform. This set up gave Certs the opportunity for increased use of his whistle. After his ceremonial inspection Certs would disperse his troops to stand at parade rest for the arrival of a train. If Certs observed the light from an arriving train on the opposite platform he would blow his whistle and motion for his crew to move to the other side of the platform.

Four trains had been inspected by his crew of ten, and so far, no one had objected to any police actions to the point where the white glove treatment had to be administered. At 9:45 a #6 local train screeched around the curve and entered the station. From his assigned post at the next to last car, Kevin

Morrow broke the most important rule of Certs Eckhart - he lost his composure. Kevin didn't just lose composure, he was going absolutely nuts, screaming at the top of his lungs. "Sergeant! Sgt. Eckhart! Oh my God. Come quickly!"

Before certs could reinstruct Kevin on maintaining a professional demeanor, he saw the reason for his uncharacteristic outburst.

Thirty-three-year-old Freddy Barnes was a subway veteran, having ridden trains almost every day for the past twenty years. Freddy had evolved as a subway rider over time. After years of being stuffed into the car with the rest of the sardines, Freddy discovered the tranquil world of riding between cars. No longer did Freddy have to push his way into a crowded car. When the train stopped at the platform, Freddy would unhook the safety chain and jump in between the cars. He had his own little world between cars where he could enjoy the ride and smoke a cigarette without disturbance from the masses. Of course, it was illegal to ride between cars, but Freddy didn't care. It was also dangerous, but Freddy always considered that the danger applied to amateurs, not professionals like himself. Freddy's craft had progressed to the point that he no longer had to wait for the train to make a complete stop before hopping onto the platform. Once the train entered the station, Freddy would unhook the safety chain and just before the train came to a complete stop he would hop to the platform. Freddy was extremely confident in his train hopping abilities, and he never had a problem - until this night.

Certs Eckhart entered full commander mode as he stared at the surreal scene. "Ok, I want an 8-man perimeter around this scene now! Kevin and Joe are on me, and the rest of you keep these people back!"

Like a finely tuned engine, the white gloved troops formed a semi-circle around the stationery subway car and began slowly walking forward, warning curious onlookers back as they progressed.

With the area secure, Certs decided to take advantage of a teaching moment for his remaining two white glovers. "Kevin, Joe," he began. "This is a rare opportunity for you. Throughout your career you will hear about a 'space case' but it's very rare to actually see one."

Certs pointed down to the platform edge while Kevin and Joe nodded like good attentive students. Certs walked to the area between cars and then back to where Freddy was stuck. "You see," Certs explained. "When he jumped off the train, he lost his footing and got caught between the platform and the moving train - a classic space case."

Whether Certs realized it or not, Freddy Barnes was conscious and breathing heavily from his pinned position. "Help me, please," he begged.

"What can we do for him?" Joe asked.

Certs shrugged. "Not much. That's the amazing thing about a space case." Certs crouched and pointed to Freddy's torso area, disregarding his pleas and continuing his lecture. "The victim is essentially cut in half, but his torso is sealed between the platform and the train." Certs pulled out his flashlight and shined it in the small space adjacent to Freddy's body. "See," Certs advised. "the lower half of his body is gone."

"Oh, yeah," Kevin stroked his chin and Joe scratched his head as they absorbed the professor's lecture. Freddy Barnes simply wept. "My legs aren't gone. I can feel them."

Certs continued to ignore the victim while addressing his men. "That's a very common reaction. Amputees often say they can still fell limbs that are no longer attached."

"So, what do we do for him, sarge?"

Certs stood up and returned his flashlight to its holder on his belt. "Like I said - nothing. As soon as the train moves the seal is broken and all his guts spill out."

"No, no, "Freddy moaned. "There has to be something you can do for me."

Certs crouched again, and for the first time addressed Freddy directly. "Sorry, but I'm just being straight with you, buddy. Once your guts spill out, you go out of the picture." Certs smiled slightly. "Look at the bright side. It will be quick."

One of Certs white gloved perimeter approached. "EMRU is here, sarge"

Certs stood again. "Good. Don't worry buddy, it won't be long now."

EMRU was the designation for the Emergency Medical Rescue Unit, the transit police equivalent to the NYPD's Emergency Service Unit. Two EMRU cops entered the perimeter and deployed their equipment. Certs knew exactly what they would do. EMRU possessed hydraulic lifts that looked like deflated balloons. These super-strong lifts could be inserted in the small space between the platform and car and when inflated the device could lift the car twelve inches.

The taller EMRU cop tapped certs on the shoulder. "We're ready to deploy the lift, sarge. Is there anything else you want to communicate to the victim before we lift the car off him?"

Certs scratched his forehead. The EMRU cop's offer provided him with the opportunity to show a little empathy to Freddy's plight. Certs crouched again and placed his right hand on Freddy's shoulder. "They are getting ready to move the car off you. Are there any last words you'd like to tell me?"

Freddy looked up at Certs through quivering lips and moist eyes. "Go fuck yourself!"

Tuesday: 10:00 pm - 18th Street

For Paddy McGrath, being out of his midnight shift comfort zone could not have worked out better. Sgt. Kelly was on the road in the lower sector during the beginning of the shift, and as Paddy had anticipated, Kelly visited him at Christopher Street for his 4:45pm revenue escort.

All subway stations had a 24-hour token booth, but there were many part time booths that only operated during certain hours. Whenever a part-time booth was going to open, the railroad clerk would go on duty at the full-time booth, pick up necessary tokens, revenue, and paperwork, and then walk to the booth to be opened. This walk was always a potentially vulnerable time since the clerk was carrying tokens and cash. Most of these booth openings were listed on roll call assignments as revenue escorts. In this case, Paddy McGrath was required to report to the main booth at Christopher Street at 4:45 to escort the clerk to the other booth on the station. Since everyone, including the sergeant, knew exactly where Paddy would be at 4:45, revenue escorts were the perfect time for the sergeant to visit the cop and sign his memo book, known as "giving a scratch."

Paddy welcomed Ron Kelly's scratch because he realized that the sergeant's visit was the last time he would see him during the shift, and he could now focus on his usual patrol activity – sleeping.

Paddy was no fool. After the escort, he visited every station on his post and made sure to say hello to the railroad clerk in each token booth. When he completed his greeting at South Ferry, he turned around and took the uptown train to 18th Street. At the north end of the uptown platform Paddy knew there was a signal room that met his specifications. The room was relatively clean, had a TA phone inside, and had strong heating pipes that were perfect anchorage points for his hammock.

By 6:15pm Paddy was settled in for his slumber. When Paddy McGrath slept, he went all in. There were no half-hearted efforts at naps with one eye open while sitting slumped in an uncomfortable chair. Paddy needed to be comfortable to sleep. Comfort included the use of his rope hammock, but there was no way to get comfortable wearing his gun belt. And who could sleep restfully in clothing, no less a police uniform. Paddy neatly placed his uniform shirt and trousers on the desk in the room. He laid his gun belt on top of his uniform and placed his shoes on the floor under the desk. Decked out only in his white t-shirt, boxer shorts, and black uniform socks, Paddy settled into the hammock for a blissful sleep.

Paddy had his logistics so well figured out that when his 9pm meal period arrived, he only had to reach his arm out of the hammock to grab the phone to call District 4 to let the assistant desk officer know that he was on meal. An hour later he completed the same process to call back from meal. The only imperfect element to this otherwise perfect evening on patrol were Paddy's kidneys. Once called back from meal he still had a good hour of snooze time, but nature was calling him.

The nearest locked employee bathroom was at the other end of the platform. Paddy sighed in his hammock. He was so comfortable he did not want to move, but unless he wanted to pull his boxers down, turn over and pee right through his hammock onto the floor, he had to get up and visit the bathroom.

Paddy stared at his uniform and equipment on the desk. He did not want to get dressed so early, but he couldn't walk down the platform in his underwear and socks. He settled on a compromise. He stepped into his trousers and his shoes. He reached for the door, but then thought better of his decision and returned to the desk. Paddy didn't want to put on his entire gun belt, but instead, removed his service revolver from its holster and shoved the 4-inch gun into his pants pocket. As he strolled down the platform in his white t-shirt and blue pants, Paddy figured he looked no different than any other subway rider.

Doris Mathis was nervous. Doris tended to be nervous about most things in life but she was

138

especially nervous whenever she had to pull her wheels. Like any other railroad clerk, Doris was required to periodically leave the safety of her token booth with bucket in hand to empty tokens from the turnstiles and bring them back inside the booth. This task was known as pulling the wheels.

Doris always felt extremely nervous when pulling the wheels and she liked to wait until she saw a police officer on the station before leaving the booth. On this night, however, she had not seen a police officer in many hours and she was almost out of tokens. Like it or not, she was going to have to grab her bucket and leave the booth.

Jim Bondi was agitated. It had to be the one week that the midnight sergeant did not have Paddy McGrath for his car-pool that the battery on his Toyota died. Jim's wife gave him a ride to the train station and an hour and a half later, he waited on the downtown #1 train platform at Penn Station for the train that would take his to 14th Street. Of course, Paddy McGrath had nothing to do with the demise of his battery, but he still couldn't help but feel some resentment toward the target of his midnight hunting expeditions.

18th Street was quiet at night to begin with, but Doris waited for an especially lifeless time when not a person could be seen within her field of view. Then, she cautiously exited her booth and approached the turnstiles. The bucket made a loud metallic sound when it landed on the concrete next to the first turnstile. Doris squinted as she bent her upper body to see the numbers on the meter on top of the turnstile. She grabbed the pen from behind her ear and copied the numbers onto the sheet on her clipboard. She took a deep breath as she grabbed the key that was attached by a chain to the clipboard and squatted next to the turnstile. She inserted the key into the door at the bottom of the turnstile and pulled the door open. Doris removed the tray from the turnstile and dumped its contents into the bucket. The sound of the tokens pouring into the bucket masked the approaching footsteps. The first indication Doris received that she was not alone was the hard, cold, steel object touching her right ear. She instinctively turned her head to the right as her eyes opened to the size of silver dollars. Doris didn't notice anything about the person. She couldn't even say if it was a man or a woman. The only object her widened eyes could focus on was the barrel of the gun pointed directly at her forehead.

Not a word had been exchanged between Doris and the gun holder when Paddy McGrath strode into the turnstile area, his walking pace a bit more purposeful as his need to empty his bladder became more urgent.

Paddy took in the scene at the turnstile and froze. "What the fuck?" he yelled.

"Help me!" Doris shouted in response.

Paddy tugged several times at his right pants pocket before his revolver finally emerged. "Police, don't move!" he bellowed.

The command did no good. The gunman, a local junkie looking for money to indulge his heroin habit, had flown up the stairs before Paddy's gun had cleared his pants.

Paddy approached Doris. "Are you alright?"

Doris took deep deliberate breaths and placed her hand on her chest. "Yes, I think so." She looked at the stairway where the perpetrator had fled. "Aren't you going after him?"

Paddy shrugged. "What's the point. He's long gone by now. Anyway, he didn't get anything and no one got hurt, right?"

"I guess so," Doris replied. "But I still better call this in to my supervisor."

Paddy smiled and held his right hand up in the universal sign for stop. "Let's think about this for a moment. If you call in an attempted booth holdup you're going to be doing paperwork for days."

"Really?" Doris responded.

"That's right." Paddy nodded. "And since so many booth holdups end up with the railroad clerk being involved, Internal Affairs will interrogate you, and they are also going to send you for a drug and alcohol test." Paddy raised an eyebrow. "You don't need all that nonsense, do you?"

"I guess not," Doris sighed.

Paddy breathed a sigh of relief. He had conveniently omitted informing Doris that his main reason to shitcan the entire incident was so that he didn't have to explain what he was doing running around the platform in his t-shirt with his gun in his pocket.

As Paddy completed his brainwashing session at the uptown turnstiles, a downtown #1 train entered the station. Jim Bondi had pulled the NY Post out of a trash can at Penn Station and was now paging through the newspaper. He was lucky McNasty Edwards was not present to see his serious violation of transit rules. As the doors closed and the train slowly began rolling forward, Jim dropped the paper slightly as he turned a page. He was startled by the scene in his field of view. He jumped out of the seat and moved to the opposite side of the car, trying desperately to get a good look before the train completely left the station. Was he hallucinating, or was that Paddy McGrath standing by the uptown turnstiles wearing a white t-shirt and uniform pants, waving his service revolver in his hand.

When the train entered the tunnel, Jim considered pulling the emergency stop cord, but realized what a horrible idea that would be. Instead, he exited the train at 14th street and waited for the L train that would take him to Union Square. He couldn't wait to be inside District 4 when Paddy McGrath arrived at the end of the 3rd platoon.

Wednesday: 2:45 pm, Union Square.

The black Chevy Caprice had not moved on 14th Street for three cycles of the traffic signal. An ambulance had all but one lane blocked bringing the normally heavy traffic to complete gridlock.

Herby Dowdle patiently tapped a rhythm on the steering wheel and waited for a chance to move. Deputy Chief George Hall was not quite as patient.

"Will you move, for Christ's sake. Why do you think you have a siren?"

The chief didn't wait for Herby to act. Instead, he reached over and pressed the center of the steering wheel, the manual means of operating the siren. "Now, go around these assholes, you asshole!"

"Yes sir, yes sir," Herby gulped as he maneuvered the car partially on the sidewalk.

When Herby was finally able to pass the ambulance, a male was being placed on a stretcher. It was obvious from the volume of blood that the man was seriously injured.

"Asshole," Chief Hall grumbled as the Caprice passed the injured man. "He's got some nerve, tying up traffic like that."

"You're absolutely right, Chief," Herby nodded.

"Of course, I'm right," the chief bellowed. "I don't need you to tell me."

Herby pulled into the police parking area on Union Square West. The police parking was no different than the rest of the parking around Union Square – there wasn't a space to be found.

"Stop here!" The chief commanded. "This is fine."

Herby obeyed, but was bewildered. "Excuse me Chief, but if I leave the car here I'll be blocking a car in."

Chief Hall pointed to the markings on the pavement. "Do you see whose car you're blocking?"

Herby strained his neck in order to see COMMANDING OFFICER printed in worn yellow paint.

The chief smiled. "That asshole Morris isn't going anywhere – now lock it up and let's go downstairs to the district."

Chief Hall walked quickly, taking huge strides. His pace was such that Herby had to break into a trot to keep up. As the chief got within twenty feet of the door to District 4 Herby had to make a quick sprint to pass his boss and open the door. Herby yanked open the door and announced the chief's presence with a high-pitched shriek. "ATTEN – SHUN!"

All members of the service were required to rise to the position of attention whenever a member in the rank above captain entered the room, but George Hall was the only high-ranking member of the transit police department who had his own private PA system to announce his arrival.

Sgt. Sean Fallon and Police Officer Lenny Alito rose unenthusiastically behind the District 4 desk. Chief Hall provided no greeting nor did he stop to sign the district blotter. Instead he turned left and continued his rapid pace past the administrative area until he reached the commanding officer's office.

Chief Hall opened the door without knocking, catching Captain Morris in the act of slurping chicken soup into his mouth, and surprising him to the point that most of the spoonful of hot soup ended up on his shirt.

"I'm not interrupting your lunch, am I Morris?" Chief Hall plopped into the chair across from the captain's desk.

"No, no… not at all Chief," Arnold stammered as he wiped his shirt with a napkin. "Can I get you anything?"

"No, I have my own lackie." George turned toward the door. "Hey you!"

Herby leaped out of the chair in the roll call area and raced toward the captain's door. He felt good about the manner in which he was summoned because the chief usually called him with *Hey asshole or Come here douchebag,* so Hey *You* was positive and may indicate that the chief was in a better mood.

Herby stuck his head in the door. "Yes sir?"

"Get me a slice of pizza upstairs."

"Right away, sir."

Herby closed the door, but could hear the chief's parting shot. "And that slice better not be cold, douchebag!"

Herby sighed as he passed the district desk. So much for the chief being in a good mood.

Chief Hall leaned forward and placed his elbows on the captain's desk, resting his chin on his hands. "So, Morris, you've had plenty of time to gather the facts, so tell me exactly what happened up in the park last night."

Arnold Morris rocked side to side in his chair and cleared his throat several times. "Well, you see Chief, it's like this." Arnold placed his outstretched arms above his head and began moving his hands slowly towards each other. "It was like several different clouds moving towards each other, and these clouds converged over Union Square Park."

Chief Hall swatted the stapler off the captain's desk, sending it flying into the wall. "Since when did you become some kind of half assed meteorologist," he bellowed. "Now spare me your screwed-up weather report and tell me what happened."

The captain was visibly shaking, which made the chief very happy. Arnold gulped down some water and took a deep breath. "What I am trying to say, Chief, is that with our people already in the park, the problem developed from two girls, some break dancers, and a disgruntled former transit cop."

George Hall sat back in the chair and stroked his chin with his right hand. For the first time in a very long time, he didn't know what to say.

THE CONVENTION

The ritual had become all too familiar. Certs Eckhart had prepared a schedule, and on this night, it was the TPF unit from District 1 who was responsible to bring the beer to the convention.

At 11:50 pm D-Day Hoffman was already in the park. Downstairs, the 3rd Platoon was ready to burst through the district door. The shift did not officially end until midnight, but the cops had the contractual right to ten minutes wash up time. At the end of every tour, cops from posts all over the district would begin assembling at Union Square about twenty minutes before shift end, slowly working their way toward the command in order to begin filing through the door at exactly ten minutes before the hour.

The District 4 personnel who were regular convention attendees slowly changed into their civilian clothing. There was no big hurry to get upstairs and into the park. The District 1 contingent who were bringing the beer would take about fifteen minutes to get down to Union Square from Midtown.

Lexi Crosby was the first to leave District 4 because she has a pitstop to make. Lexi was trying to rehabilitate her reputation in the district, so her detour to the 24-hour deli on Union Square East to pick of two six packs of beer certainly didn't hurt her public relations campaign.

Certs led his obedient TPF minions into the park like a mother duck parading in front of her ducklings. Ace Styles and Willie Dewar strolled into the park while carrying on a lively debate. Ace believed there was a fifty-fifty chance the girls they met at Chambers Street earlier would seek them out in the park after they left their party. Willie thought Ace was crazy, and that it was at best a ten percent chance the girls would materialize.

Mike Galante was still seething. From the time they had departed 8th Street after responding to the 10-13 right up until he sat on a bench in the middle of Union Square Park, Mike had only one subject on his mind.

"I'm going to call the Amateur Bowlers Association of America," he declared.

Eddie McDaniel chuckled. "Go ahead, I'm sure they could use a good laugh."

Mike pointed his finger at his partner. "This is no laughing matter. I got screwed."

"Screwed?" Eddie shrieked. "Why don't you just appreciate what you accomplished. Not many bowlers can say they rolled strikes in nine straight frames."

Mike shook his head. "That's not the point."

Eddie held up his hand. "I'm not finished. And I don't know if any other bowlers have ever rolled strikes for the first nine frames and then thrown a gutter ball in the tenth frame." Eddie almost fell off the bench trying to control his laughter.

"Asshole," Mike growled. "Lane 1 is warped, and you know it. I bowled nine frames on lane 28 and I should have been allowed to finish the game on 28."

Eddie held his arms out to the side. "So why did you bowl on lane 1?"

"Don't be stupid," Mike warned. "You were there. Gino said we weren't going to be able to get back on 28 for at least two hours."

"So, why did you bowl on lane 1?"

Mike bit his lip. "Because it was the only lane available."

"Yeah," Eddie nodded. "It was available because it's warped."

"That's my point," Mike crowed.

Eddie was confused. "What point? What do you want that bowling organization to do for you?"

"I want a ruling," Mike stated. "I want to be able to go back to the bowling alley and bowl the tenth frame of the game on lane 28, like I should have."

Eddie wore a wide grin. "You can do that anyway, partner. I'll go with you tomorrow."

Mike wagged his finger and shook his head. "It's not that simple. I want the organization to officially sanction what I am doing so that I can legitimately tell my grandchildren that I bowled a perfect game."

Eddie slapped Mike's back. "Good luck. If the bowling organization won't help you, maybe we can get the Supreme Court to take the case."

Mike sighed. "Where's the beer?"

One of the benefits of working the home post at Union Square was the ability to take personal breaks inside District 4 instead of some dark, dank, dirty porter's room. That's exactly what Billy Normile had done at 11:15 pm. He entered the district and notified the desk officer that he was going to the men's room near the locker rooms. While Billy took care of his business at the urinal he heard the very loud, excited voice of sergeant Jim Bondi just outside the bathroom door. Bondi was telling another sergeant how he had just seen Paddy McGrath walking on the platform at 18th Street in his underwear. Billy completed his mission at the urinal, but he remained inside the bathroom. He wanted to hear the rest of the sergeant's story. Bondi was gleeful in saying that after all the time he spent hunting for McGrath on the midnight shift he finally got him on the 3rd platoon. Bondi said he was going to wait at the district desk for the 3rd platoon to enter the command at 11:50 and then swoop down on Paddy, take him into the captain's office, interrogate him and get him to admit that he was out of uniform while on duty.

When the voices had faded in the distance, Billy exited the bathroom and returned to the mezzanine outside District 4. He strolled over to the stairway to the L train because he knew that was the location where Paddy McGrath would rise from on his return trip to the command.

At 11:40 Billy was startled by a voice from behind him. "What's up Billy boy?"

Billy Normile nodded and smiled. "I'll tell you what's up, Paddy boy."

Billy explained Sgt. Bondi's plan, while Paddy took it all in, stroking his chin with his right hand. "I'll tell you what, Billy," Paddy began. "At 11:50, you enter the district with the rest of the guys. Go to the back of the locker room and open the emergency door."

"But the alarm will sound," Billy warned.

Paddy shook his head. "There's a box next to the alarm bell. Open the box and pull the fuse. That will silence the alarm. Open the door and let me in, and I'll change quickly and go out the same way."

"No problem, Paddy. But you're still gonna have to deal with Bondi next week when you're back on midnights, right?"

Paddy held up one hand. "I'll deal with next week when it arrives. Besides, that putz will likely have forgotten about this by then."

At 11:50 Billy Normile was the first cop through the district door. As he tossed his memo book in the wooden box on the desk he couldn't help but notice Sgt. Bondi standing behind the desk officer. He looked like a drooling lion waiting to pounce on a zebra.

Billy quickly made his way through the locker room to the emergency door. He had his hand on the crash bar when he remembered the alarm. He opened the box next to the bell and pulled out the fuse, then he pushed hard on the door and ushered a waiting Paddy McGrath into the locker room. Five minutes later Paddy was about to exit through the same door, but his escape was halted by Father Frank Mullins.

"Paddy, wait," Father Frank gasped.

Paddy made a quick about face in the doorway. Father Frank caught his breath and explained the situation. "Bondi is really pissed. He knows you're trying to avoid him so he just ran upstairs to wait by your car."

"Thanks, Frank."

"What are you gonna do?" Frank asked.

Paddy smiled. "I'm gonna wait him out."

"How are you gonna do that?"

"He has to go on patrol sometime. I'm gonna take a slow walk to Union Square West, grab a beer at the deli, and go hang out at the convention until the prick leaves."

Little by little the nightly convention came together. The District 1 TPF boys arrived with the beer to the cheers of the thirsty cops seated on benches in the middle of the park.

The gatherings had developed into a routine with assigned seating. Certs and his TPF contingent sat around in an open grassy area adjacent to the main walkway. This location was perfect for Certs to make speeches and tell tales to his disciples. The District 4 attendees hung out just to the west of Certs' turf on a cluster of benches that surrounded concrete tables with chess boards built in. No one ever played chess, but the tables served a purpose and were usually filled with bottles and cans at the end of a meeting. All the District 4 regulars were on the benches. D-Day

Hoffman had already been there for forty-five minutes waiting for the end of the 3rd platoon. Ace Styles and Willie Dewar picked a bench where they could see out to Union Square East. They wanted to be in a position to see their lady friends approaching so they could quickly run out of the park to cut them off at the pass if they saw them about to descend into the subway. Husky and Starch were perched on top of a bench, slurping beers while Mike Galante continued to rant about his bowling catastrophe.

This was Paddy McGrath's first convention. His midnight shift was usually just beginning when the park festivities began, but on this night, he had to stay in the park. He squinted to look out to the police parking area on Union Square East. Sgt. Bondi was still pacing back and forth behind Paddy's car. *Oh well,* Paddy thought as he took another sip of beer.

Father Frank Mullins and Doctor Dolan were intermittent convention attendees, but on this beautiful summer night they were on the benches. Father Frank had convinced the doctor to attend, either to counsel him regarding his toss of the man into the trash can or to congratulate him.

Larry Legend Holland already had established a convention routine. He attended regularly but was always the first to leave. Larry would quietly sit on the benches for one beer so that he could unwind and momentarily forget about all the stress in his life at home. As soon as he drained his beer, Larry would quietly slip away.

Lexi Crosby was becoming a convention regular. She had become so unpopular because of her big mouth on patrol, and the incident at Broad Street with her former boyfriend had made her something of a laughing stock. Lexi was working overtime to rehabilitate her reputation, beginning with showing up at the convention every night with two six packs of beer.

Angelo Petrino was a first timer at the convention. Angelo had no desire to hang out with these burnt out hairbags, but his earlier conversation with Lexi at Broadway – Lafayette had piqued his curiosity. Maybe Ken and Barbie would produce gorgeous children and maybe that production process could begin in a secluded area of the park.

Johnny Alphabets strolled into the park a few minutes after everyone else. He had to wait for JoJo Palermo to tell him to return to the District in the RMP and then John had to inspect the car before he could go off duty. Johnny was the most enthusiastic conventioneer. Sometimes he would sit in the grass among the TPF faction, and at other times he took up a position on the District 4 benches. During a typical night Johnny would bounce around between groups three or four times.

McNasty Edwards was also a regular with a routine. He was as miserable off duty as he was on duty. Joe sat at his own bench and drank the free beer, socializing with no one and only blurting out an insult or a snide remark when he picked up something in an adjacent conversation.

...

The heart of NYC beats constantly, sometimes at a very loud, rapid pace. For the cops of District 4, however, the beat of the city was so familiar that it had become imperceptible. – they didn't feel it anymore. It crept up on them on this summer night until they looked up from their beer.....and one spark, from the most unlikely source, and Union Square Park was on fire.

At 1:30 AM the clouds referenced by Captain Morris began converging on the park. The first cloud began drifting in from the east. The Regal Ballroom was usually inactive on a weeknight. The only time there was activity from the banquet hall located just east of Union Square was for weekend wedding receptions and organizational dinners. On this night, however, the clouds were assembling in the form of the New York City Breakdancing Championships.

Breakdancing was an athletic style of street dance created by the African American youth in the early 1970s. By the late seventies, the dance had begun to spread to other communities and was gaining wider popularity.

The breakdancing craze quickly gripped the nation, and particularly in large cities like New York. The 1984 World B-boy Battle Championships were held on this hot summer night inside the Regal Ballroom.

In the wee hours of the morning the first cloud had formed perfectly. The crowd of highly energized urban youth had departed the Regal Ballroom and were making their way across Union Square Park to the subway entrance. By itself, this cloud would not have been enough to ignite a storm. The band of hopped up kids would have passed the drinking cops without incident.

Enter cloud number two from the west. It was Johnny Alphabets who first took note of the duo as he moved from the District 4 benches to the TPF assembly. "Oh boy," he declared. "Those two look like they had a few too many."

Johnny's declaration drew everyone's attention, but it was Ace Styles and Willie Dewar who were particularly interested.

In the glare from the streetlights their make-up looked clownish, their hair was a mess, and their cheeks were flushed red. One had what appeared to be wine stains running down the front of her dress as they both unsteadily staggered across the street.

Maybe she just misjudged the curb, or maybe she just tripped in her drunken stupor. Either way, the younger of the duo remained prone at the edge of the sidewalk while her older friend urged her to get up.

"Oh my God!" Willie exclaimed.

"Jesus Christ," Ace stated. "I was hoping they'd be a little liquored up, but this is ridiculous."

As Ace and Willie began walking to the edge of the park to check on the condition of their new friends, there was already activity taking place around the ladies. A group of passing break dancers was getting a hearty laugh out of the plight of the two drunks, and the older woman was not amused by the joviality of the group.

"What are you laughing at?" she slurred. "You're all nothing but animals who belong in the zoo."

The woman reared back an unleashed an open hand slap that landed on a tall lean Hispanic teenager.

"What the hell, lady," the teen yelled as he reached forward and pushed her away. The force of the push drove her back and she fell backwards over her face down friend.

The laughter gained in volume until Willie grabbed the teen by the collar. "You like assaulting women," he snarled. "Why don't you try that with me?"

The kid broke free from Willie's grasp. "I didn't assault no one, man. That drunk lady assaulted me."

The groups had formed around the fallen drunken women. On one side were the convention cops and on the other were the break dancing kids. There was posturing and threats. Both sides were poised for combat. It would only take one more spark to ignite all hell to break loose, but thankfully, there was a fireman among all the cops.

D-Day Hoffman moved between the two groups. "Ok, everyone, calm down." He pointed down to the women. "Obviously, these ladies have had a little too much to drink, and I think we should get them some help." The calm, grandfatherly image of the retired cop seemed to have a de-escalating effect on the break dancers

D-Day looked at the teen who had been slapped. "There's no problem here, right?"

The teen shook his head. "No problem."

"Good," D-Day replied as he leaned down to help the older woman to her feet. "Then we'll help these fine ladies and you all can have a good night."

The teens began descending into the subway while D-Day continued lifting the older woman to her feet. "Anyone know these two?" he groaned as he scanned the assembled cops.

Ace and Willie shuffled their feet and nervously looked at the ground. They weren't about to claim these two drunks.

Johnny Alphabets lifted the younger woman to her feet and the ladies held onto each other as they tried to figure out where they were. Suddenly, the younger women's drunken haze momentarily lifted as she recognized a familiar face. She pointed a quivering finger toward Ace. "Hey, there you are. I bet you're surprised we took you up on your invitation."

Ace bit his lip and shrugged. "Surprised really doesn't cover how I feel right now," he mumbled.

Certs approached Ace. "You know these two?" he asked.

"Of course, he knows us," the young woman babbled. "He and that black guy invited us here."

Certs moved his icy stare back and forth between Ace and Willie. Before Certs could make any speech, the older woman made an observation. "Hey," she yelled while pointing at Ace. "What happened to you, your dick is not big anymore?"

The earlier laughter from the break dancers was nothing compared to the roar erupting in the park. Ace turned four different shades of red but said nothing. There was nothing to say – the damage was done, and Ace knew this would be permanent damage. The story of a woman declaring that he no longer had a big dick in front of a large group of cops was not going away – ever!

D-Day still held the older woman by the arm as he looked to Ace and Willie. "You can't let them go into the subway in this condition. You better keep them here for a while."

Billy Normile specifically addressed Ace. "D-Day's right, needle dick, you better bring them over to the benches."

Ace grabbed the older woman's arm while Willie took control of the younger lady. The older woman was babbling non-stop on the short walk to the benches, but Ace didn't hear a thing. There were only two words on his mind – words that he knew he would be hearing for the rest of his career – needle dick.

A degree of normalcy had returned to the convention. Certs and his TPF boys had returned to their grassy knoll, while the District 4 crew began to fill the benches. Ace led his lady toward a vacant bench, but when she got about six paces from the seat she doubled over, vomit splashing on the pavement and spraying on Ace's new designer jeans.

The laughter reached a new crescendo as Ace shook his head and wondered what else could happen to him. His answer would be forthcoming directly.

The laughter suddenly ceased with the sound of the siren and the visual of the blue and red light moving rapidly across the park. The third cloud had arrived. Alone, most clouds are benign and don't pose a threat. A cumulus cloud, however, can be the originator of severe storms. This dense, towering vertical cloud is carried by powerful upward air currents. This night's cumulus cloud was not carried by air currents – it was carried inside an NYPD RMP, and it had a different name. This storm generating cumulus cloud was named Tony Regina.

Tony Regina hated transit cops, which was odd considering Tony had been a transit cop. In 1981 Tony had been appointed to the Transit Police Department and spent two years assigned to District 4. During his time with Transit, there was no bigger booster of the department. There were many nights at Kate Cassidy's Pub in Queens when Tony would invite an NYPD cop out to Woodhaven Blvd. to discuss a disparaging remark made regarding the transit police.

Just before he had been appointed a transit police officer, Tony had taken the NYPD exam, and two years after he was on the job with transit he was offered appointment to the NYPD. Suddenly, Tony's attitude made a complete reversal. As soon as he completed the "rollover" training at the police academy for transit and housing cops changing over to the NYPD, transit cops were suddenly lowlife scum and the NYPD was the greatest thing since sliced bread. He was assigned to the 13th Precinct, the NYPD command covering Union Square.

McNasty Edwards referred to Tony as a wannabe tough guy and an arrogant punk. When informed that Tony had rolled over to the NYPD, Joe's only response was "good riddance." The rest of the cops did not share McNasty's over the top negative sentiments, but no one shed a tear at Tony's departure. Billy Normile summed up the majority opinion of Tony Regina. "He's a douchebag – but he's harmless."

Tony was well aware of the Union Square Park conventions, and whenever he was working a midnight tour, he would make sure to drive into the park to do a little ball breaking. The last time he made an appearance he slowly drove past the drinking transit cops with his window rolled down while commenting to his partner as loud as possible. "I used to be one of those loser drunken transit cops."

One of Certs Eckhart's white gloved troopers threw a beer can that hit Tony's RMP, prompting Tony to step out of the car and go into his tough guy act.

The curtain came down very quickly on Tony's act when he recognized that his 5'9", 160-pound frame was going to have a problem intimidating the 6'5" 260-pound TPF cop. Even McNasty Edwards laughed when Tony leaped back in his car and sped out of the park.

Tony turned off the siren as he stopped his RMP next to the benches. He got out of the car and swaggered over to the benches where the drunk ladies were seated. "Well, well," Tony grinned. "You losers have done it now."

Eddie McDaniel responded for the group. "What are you talking about, Regina?"

"A job just came over the air that a couple of females were being assaulted in Union Square Park." Tony shook his head. "I should have known it was you clowns."

"So now you know," Mike Galante added. "So why don't you be on your way, Regina."

"Oh no!" Tony wagged his finger. "You guys don't get it. I have complainants here, and if they want to press charges, I'm gonna collar some of you boys."

Doctor Dolan sat alone on the eastern-most bench staring up at the moon. "Did you hear that ma?" he sang. "He's gonna collar us – how do you like that, ma?" The Doctor than cupped his hands around his mouth and screamed at the top of his lungs, "ASSHOLE!"

Tony turned toward the scream. "What did you say?"

McNasty Edwards approached from behind and tapped Tony on his shoulder. "Hey punk, why don't you hit the road."

Tony spun around and took a quick step toward Joe Edwards. His feet landed directly in the woman's slippery vomit, and two seconds later Tony Regina was lying on his back in a pile of puke.

Ace Syles could take some solace in the fact that the level of laughter resulting from Tony Regina's slip and fall had easily surpassed the volume for his small dick remark.

Tony scrambled to his feet and reached for his handcuff case. "You're under arrest, Edwards."

"No, you're under arrest, Regina," McNasty growled.

Tony Regina's partner for the shift, Martin Sloan, was a rookie three weeks removed from the Police Academy. During the entire interaction Martin had stood by the passenger door and watched. Now, as Tony and McNasty began shoving each other, Martin took his first action. He grabbed his radio and put it up to his mouth. "10-13 Union Square Park. Officer needs assistance forthwith."

For an instant time seemed to stand still. Everyone, including the grappling Tony Regina and McNasty Edwards stopped what they were doing and stared at Martin Sloan. No one could believe he had just called a 10-13, the most serious emergency call a police officer could make.

Time resumed with the sounds of the sirens approaching the park from all directions. A total of eight NYPD RMPs were strewn over the grass and roadway in the center of the park. One sergeant and fifteen cops faced off against the transit police conventioneers. For a while it appeared that cooler heads would prevail. Certs and the NYPD sergeant held back their forces and it looked as if the episode would end as a non-incident.

The cumulus cloud named Tony Regina wouldn't move away, and he didn't realize how unpredictable and dangerous a tornado is, especially a tornado named Doctor Dolan.

Certs and the NYPD sergeant had shaken hands and were beginning to move their men away from each other. Everyone seemed to be satisfied with the result of the incident – everyone except Tony Regina. "This is bullshit," Tony lamented. He waved his arms towards the transit contingent. "They're nothing but a bunch of wannabe cops." Tony happened to catch Joe Dolan in his field of view. "And Dolan is the sickest bitch in their whole sick tribe."

Doctor Dolan calmly walked in the direction of Tony Regina. Father Frank Mullins looked at the ground and shook his head. He mumbled to Larry Holland, "I wish he hadn't said that."

In an encore performance from earlier in the evening at West 4th Street, Doctor Dolan wrapped his arms around a stunned Tony Regina, lifted him off his feet, and deposited him in a litter basket. As with the prior 10-13 call, for a moment, everything seemed to stop. Then, as if the bell had been rung to start a boxing round, the battle was on.

The NYPD was badly outnumbered, so the sergeant called for a Level 1 mobilization, resulting in the response of the Manhattan South Task Force to even the odds a bit. The battle had evolved into a cluster of individual scuffles. Certs Eckhart turned the tide in transit's favor with one blow of his whistle. Certs TPF squad broke free from their clashes and fell in behind Certs.

Certs turned to his men and shouted. "To a wedge, move!"

The TPF commandos formed an inverted V and waited for Certs' next command. "Charge!" he roared.

Like a human lawn mower, the TPF wedge began mowing down the NYPD. The only non-combatants were sitting on the transit benches. The drunk women were still trying to figure out where they were. The younger one poked her friend. "Who's fighting? Are we still at the party?"

"No, silly," her older friend replied. "We're in the park with those cops we met tonight."

"What cops?" the young girl questioned.

"Don't you remember," the older woman responded. "the black guy and the guy with the big dick who turned out to have a small dick."

D-Day Hoffman could take no more of the stimulating dialogue. He took a deep breath and hopped up on top of a concrete chess table. He cupped his hands around his mouth and tried to be heard above the sound of battle. "That's enough! Everyone at ease!"

There was no response to D-Day's cry. "He took another deep breath and prepared another loud plea. Suddenly, he couldn't take the deep breath required for a shout. Then, he couldn't catch his breath at all. The sharp pain in his chest told him something was drastically wrong.

The combatants finally responded to a scream, but it was the screams of the drunken women witnessing D-Day collapse off the table that brought the brawl to an abrupt halt. More lights and sirens entered Union Square Park, but no more police vehicles arrived. This time the night was illuminated by the arrival of an ambulance.

D-Day was on his way to the emergency room while several other ambulances arrived to tend to the scraped-up brawlers. The NYPD sergeant and Certs Eckhart repeated their earlier handshake, this time as a symbolic end to the hostilities.

Certs turned away to collect all his troops, but he suddenly stopped and sighed. He observed a wrestling match still taking place in a cluster of trees. Certs called out to Billy Normile, who was the closest person to the trees. "Hey Billy, please go tell those idiots that the war is over."

Billy trotted toward the trees while everyone else began making their exit from the park.

"Holy shit!" Billy Normile's cry wasn't communicating fear or tragedy. It was more a shout of excitement and wonder. Whatever he was trying to communicate, the message he transmitted was for everyone to run and join him. Within thirty seconds a human circle had formed around the trees. There were at least two dozen other exclamations of "Holy shit" along with several other incantations of surprise and excitement.

171

Angelo Petroni was the first out of the foliage. He looked very calm and satisfied as he pulled up his trousers. As a matter of fact, Angelo appeared proud. It didn't really matter what emotions Angelo was exhibiting – no one was looking at him. Everyone was still focused on the center of the clearing. Lexi Crosby rolled around on the grass and dirt, furiously pawing the ground in an attempt to locate her clothes. She glanced at the circle of manhood enjoying her nakedness. Lexi closed her eyes and bit her lip. This was going to require a much bigger public relations campaign.

THE AFTERMATH

16th Street & 1st Avenue: 4:45am

The emergency room at Beth Israel Hospital was uncharacteristically quiet for a summer night in Manhattan. The group of eight transit cops had no problem finding seats together in one corner of the waiting room.

Ace and Willie stared straight ahead and said nothing. They liked D-Day, but the main reason they had come to the hospital was to rid themselves of the drunken girls in the park.

"I hope D-Day is Ok," Willie whispered.

"Yeah," Ace agreed." You know, in retrospect, maybe all those socks down my pants were too much."

Willie shook his head. "No, like I told you before, it was very subtle."

Johnny Alphabets stared at the black-framed wall clock for the ninth time in an hour, scrutinizing the second hand, which seemed to linger an extra minute at every passing second. He took his gaze off of the clock, silently vowing to not look at it once more until absolutely necessary and pulled out a paperback entitled *Improving My Vocabulary.* Johnny skimmed through the same words repeatedly before reluctantly glancing at the clock as the second hand continued to move in its persistent manner. His concentration was disrupted by the sudden sound of a door creaking open, and his eyes shifted to see a young nurse in her 30s stepping out. Johnny immediately rose from the edge of the chair but to his dismay, the nurse walked to the other side of the room to confer with an elderly couple. The nurse spun around on her white shoes and walked away, the rhythm of her heels clicking against the hard-concrete floor synchronizing with the ceaseless ticking of the wall clock.

After sitting in the waiting room for hours, Billy Normile believed he was near death. The clacking of the keys coming from the passing of the same security guard and the constant boring commercials from the TV was driving him insane. He wanted to know what was going on with D-Day right then, not ten minutes, two hours or forty years later; he wanted to know before his brain shut down. Billy placed his hands over his face and took a deep breath. He then watched the same commercial again.

Father Frank Mullins, Doctor Dolan, and Husky and Starch sat in a cluster of four chairs facing each other. Father Frank extended his hands to the side. "I think we should all join hands and say a Rosary for D-Day."

Eddie McDaniel continued looking at the floor. "Please shut up, Frank."

The same young nurse entered the room again. "Is anyone here for Mr. Hoffman?"

All eight transit cops stood in the corner of the waiting room. The nurse smiled. "Mr. Hoffman is going to be Ok."

Father Frank looked to the heavens. "Thank God!" he exclaimed.

Ace collapsed back in his seat, stretched and yawned. "Finally," he said. "Something good has happened tonight. Maybe things are turning around for us."

Ace thought the approaching male may have been hospital personnel with more information about D-Day. "Are you guys the transit cops from Union Square Park?" The tall thin male asked.

"Yes," Ace nodded.

"I'm Jordon Wright with the New York Post and I'd like to get a statement about the police riot tonight in Union Square Park."

Ace slumped in his seat, totally deflated. Willie smiled and sighed. "You really nailed that one Ace. Things are really looking up."

Wednesday 3:30PM

You could hear a pin drop in the District 4 muster room. Johnny Alphabets stood in the center of the assembled cops in his normal statue-like position of attention. The rest of the cops filled the ranks and made their best attempts to assume a position that looked something like attention.

Most of the cops had developed high levels of cynicism and apathy, but they weren't stupid. No one was eager to incur the wrath of the caged lion growling in front of them.

Deputy Chief George Hall paced back and forth in front of the ranks, intermittently pounding a rolled-up newspaper against his leg. Every now and then he would stop and glare at the cops, an indication that a verbal barrage was imminent. But no words came forth as the chief pounded his leg harder and resumed pacing the floor.

The assembled cops weren't the only members of District 4 on edge. Captain Arnold Morris stood near the wall in front of the formation of police officers. Arnold's nerves were at the breaking point. Every time the pacing chief made a turn in front of the group, he was walking directly at Arnold, and the captain feared an attack was imminent. Arnold breathed a sigh of relief every time the chief turned and walked away in the opposite direction, but the building pressure was too much. Arnold had to do something to calm his nerves, so he reverted to his old reliable technique – he stared at the ceiling.

Chief Hall made six more circuits in front of the troops before his expression began to change. When he began walking in the direction of Captain Morris his eyes widened and his nostrils flared. Arnold's worst fears were realized when the chief made no more turns. Instead he continued moving towards the captain. Arnold tried to ignore the approaching behemoth and remained focused on the ceiling. As Chief Hall approached, he raised the arm that was wielding the rolled-up newspaper. Like a dog-owner who discovered his pet had made on the carpet the newspaper struck hard on the side of Arnold's head.

"Stop staring at the god damn ceiling," the chief roared.

There were some muffled snickers from the ranks, but fear prevented any substantial show of hilarity.

Chief Hall menacingly pointed the newspaper at the cops. "I'm gonna say this only once. I don't ever want to hear that any of you morons have been in Union Square Park again." The chief's voice increased in volume. "I don't care if you're off duty. I don't care if your kids are being kidnapped in the park, or your wife is screwing some guy in the trees up there." The chief glared at Lexi Crosby who already had blushed through several shades.

"You stay out of the park, understand?" The chief's voice lowered to a little more than a whisper, but his message was loud and clear. "If I catch any of you assholes in that park I will personally kick the shit out of you," He moved his icy stare from face to face. "If you don't believe me – try me!"

Chief Hall unrolled his weapon and displayed the headline to the roll call. "Police riot in Union Square Park," he shook his head. "You dipshits better hope this goes away. You already have a chief who wants to put you in orange uniforms. With bullshit like this you'll end up carrying brooms instead of guns." Chief Hall slapped the headline. "Ten cops need hospital treatment in battle of the blue. What a great story," he growled as he began to leave the muster room.

"Excuse me, Chief."

There was a collective gasp in the ranks when Billy Normile's voice sounded.

George Hall stopped in the muster room doorway and turned toward the direction of the inquiry, the newspaper tightly rolled in his right hand. "What?" he bellowed.

Billy cleared his throat. "I was just wondering, chief. How many of the hospitalized cops were transit?"

The chief's eyes widened again and his grip on the newspaper tightened. "You tell me, smart guy."

Billy shrugged. "None of the injured cops were transit."

"Asshole!" Chief Hall growled.

Before the chief turned away, Billy was sure he recognized a slight smile and wink.

The traffic was horrible, but Herby Dowdle had managed to make it to the Brooklyn Bridge in a reasonable amount of time. Herby was so proud of his driving prowess that he dared to risk asking a question.

"Can I ask you something, Chief?"

There was a grunt from the passenger seat that Herby interpreted as a yes. "What was the point of that cop's question about how many transit cops were hurt in the fight? What did that matter?"

Chief Hall turned and stared at his weasel-like assistant, a look of disgust on his face. "You, and all the cowardly worms like you would never understand."

"Thank you, Chief."

HAIRBAG NATION: A Story of the New York City Transit Police

Thursday: 2:15pm 16ᵗʰ Street & 1ˢᵗ Avenue

Billy Normile had taken up the quick collection and purchased the flowers. Father Frank Mullins accompanied Billy in the elevator to the 4ᵗʰ floor.

The door to room 422 was brown and dull like all the others. A nurse smiled kindly as she opened the door wider. Doctors and nurses surrounded D-Day's hospital bed, attaching IV's, heart monitors and oxygen tanks to him. Billy and Father Frank slid through the open door and explored the room while the other people were still crowded around D-Day.

Seeing the room Billy immediately understood why people took flowers to hospital rooms. Despite medical science, there was something in our natures that required natural beauty as part of the healing process. We weren't robots, we weren't "units" to be fixed; D-Day wasn't there for a quick oil and filter change. In their efforts not to offend they succeeded in not inspiring or lifting the spirit. Billy sat next to Frank near the window and placed the flowers on the windowsill. Activity was still peaking around D-Day's bed, so Billy took a deep breath and stared up at the ceiling.

Father Frank noticed Billy's gaze. "What are you doing, taking after Captain Morris?"

Billy immediately changed his focal point. An old TV set hung from the ceiling. A window giving him a view of the world below was just beneath the screen. In the other corner were two chairs, frayed with wear and tear. It was a typical hospital room, sparse and functional.

The doctor and nurses exited the room, and the pleasant-looking woman at the bedside smiled and approached Billy and Frank.

"I'm Lorraine Hoffman," she greeted. "Do you gentlemen work with Howard."

Billy nodded. "Yes, ma'am. We work in District 4."

"Thank God he's alright," Father Frank added.

Lorraine placed her hand over her heart. "Lord, yes. What a scare this was."

Lorraine pointed to the bed. "They gave him something to help him sleep, so he's a little groggy. But you fellows go talk to him. He'll be glad to see you." Lorraine pointed to the room door. "I'm going downstairs to get a cup of coffee."

D-Day's eyes were closed when Billy and Frank approached the bed.

"D-Day," Billy whispered. "Can you hear me?"

D-Day's eyes opened. "Yeah, I'm still here," he replied.

Billy nodded. "It's good to see you, buddy."

D-Day smiled. "It's good to see you guys too."

Father Frank placed his hand on D-Day's hand. "Would you like to pray with me, D-Day?"

Billy rolled his eyes. "Come on, Frank."

"That's ok," D-Day chuckled. "I appreciate the offer, Frank, but I think I'll pass right now – maybe next time."

Billy smiled. "Hey D-Day, I have to ask you something."

"Go ahead,"

"What did your wife say when she found out you have been retired for months."

A wide grin appeared on D-Day's face. "Who said she knows I'm retired."

"What?"

"I'm out on extended sick leave until I'm well enough to return to duty."

Billy shook his head. "You're an amazing man, my friend."

D-Day sighed. "The only problem is that when I come back to duty, I'm going to have to figure out somewhere to go. From what I hear you guys are out of business with the convention."

Billy and Frank looked at each other and smiled. Billy returned his eyes to D-Day. "I don't think I'd go so far as to say the convention is out of business."

Two Weeks Later: 12:30am

Johnny Alphabets was excited. He had been on vacation since the Union Square riot, and he was amazed to learn that the convention was still taking place at a more discreet location.

Johnny bounced down the dimly lit staircase and opened the door. The smells were the first sense to kick in – the mixture of floor polish, disinfectant, stale cigarette smoke, hot dogs, and spilled beer. Then the sounds took over – balls crashing, bouncing, and rolling, pins scattering, the whirr of a ball returning through a machine, and people laughing and shouting. Finally, there were the sights – the check in counter, the racks of bowling balls, waxed wooden lanes, and ugly shoes.

The shoes. Johnny did a double-take. The anti-crime shoes were all over the place. Before he could consider what was going on with the shoes, his attention was drawn to a call from the far end of the alley.

"Johnny, over here."

Johnny squinted until he focused on Eddie McDaniel waving to him from the far end of the bowling alley.

Johnny nodded in approval as he approached the end of the alley. The last four lanes- 27-30 – were

185

occupied by the conventioneers. Certs and his TPF crew lounged in the blue and orange plastic seats in lanes 27 and 28 while the District 4 3rd platoon was strewn around lanes 29 and 30.

Most of the District 4 regulars were present. Father Frank Mullins and Doctor Dolan were at the scorer's table. Eddie McDaniel and Mike Galante sat on the plastic seats behind lane 29, while Billy Normile, Angelo Petrino and Lexi Crosby sat behind lane 30. Sitting in a chair by himself, sipping a beer behind the bowling ball racks was McNasty Edwards. Ace Styles and Willie Dewar apparently had not learned a lesson. They sat at the bar yucking it up with two inebriated females. The laughs turned to shrieks when Ace revealed his bulging crotch business card.

There was one new face at this convention. Billy Normile came up behind Johnny and began massaging his shoulders. "This is the big night, kid. The 3rd platoon is counting on you."

Johnny was more confused than usual. "What are you talking about, Billy?"

"Follow me," Billy instructed.

Billy led Johnny past the bar where the females were still admiring the huge bulge in Ace's pants. Johnny was surprised to the see the occupant of a table in the back of the bar.

Sy Goldenberg sat at the table, rotating his arms and neck. He saw Johnny approaching and smiled. "Finally, I get to teach this young buck a lesson."

Johnny turned to Billy Normile. "What's going on?"

Billy slapped Johnny's wide back. "Sgt. Goldenberg got out of his warm bed to come here and prove who is the District 4 strongman."

Johnny looked back at the table. Sy Goldenberg waited, gritting his teeth with his elbow on the table, hand open like a claw waiting for Johnny to lock up in a test of strength.

Johnny turned back to Billy. "This is ridiculous. I'm gonna let him win."

Billy shook his head vigorously. "No, no, Johnny boy, you can't do that. The pride of the 3rd platoon is at stake."

Johnny sighed and took the seat opposite Sy Goldengerg. "How's is going sarge?"

"I'm great," Sy declared. "but I won't be able to say the same thing for you in a minute."

Johnny locked hands with Sy as all the conventioneers gathered around the table. All except Ace and Willie, who were still trying to seal the deal with the drunks at the bar.

Sy's eyes widened and he began growling at Johnny. Johnny thought this was the sergeant's attempt to psyche him out, so he let Sy have his fun. After about twenty seconds of the growling, Johnny turned his head to Billy Normile. "When are we going to start?"

Sy's eyes widened. He began to feel dizzy. His mouth was dry as he gasped for air. "When do we start?" he blurted.

The truth was obvious to everyone except Johnny Alphabets. What Johnny had perceived to be a psyche-out attempt was actually Sy Goldenberg pushing against Johnny's arm for all he was worth.

Doctor Dolan brought the competition to a quick conclusion with one of his primal screams. "NOW!"

Johnny acted reflexively to the screamed command and slammed Sy's arm down hard on the wooden surface. The cheers from the onlookers masked Sy's moans of agony. From that day forward, the phone books in District 4 were safe.

Aside from the playboys at the bar, two other conventioneers had missed the arm wrestling massacre. Eddie McDaniel had accompanied Mike Galante to the front desk so he could confer with the manager.

Mike unfolded a piece of paper from his shirt pocket. "I need to show you something, Gino,"

"What is it Mike?" Gino moaned. "I'm very busy back here right now."

"It's a ruling from the Amateur Bowlers Association of America."

"A what?"

"A ruling, Gino. The association officially recognizes my right to continue my game from two weeks ago on lane 28."

Gino shrugged. "You have lane 28 tonight. So, go finish your game."

"I just want you to be aware of what I'm doing," Mike replied.

"So, now I'm aware," Gino said as he ducked under the desk to return two pair of shoes. "Knock yourself out."

"You know," Mike continued. "If I strike out in the last frame, I'll have a perfect game."

Gino extended his arms to the side. "What do you want me to do, Mike, blow a trumpet?"

Mike Galante waved his hand in disgust as he left the desk and prepared for his moment of truth.

Two strikes later, Mike stared down lane 28. He was one strike away from bowling immortality. The ball felt smooth as he rubbed his hand along the surface. He wiggled his fingers as he felt the blast of the dryer on his hands. He slowly slipped his fingers into the holes and lifted. The ball was heavy in Mike's hands as he scanned the pins. Just one more strike was all he needed. He tuned out the bass-heavy music, the kids screwing around on lane 26, the lights glaring off the alley's high sheen until all he could see was his target: the one inch-square spot to the right of the head pin.

All the conventioneers had stopped what they were doing to watch Mike's attempt for glory. Even some bowlers from other lanes had drifted over to lane 28 to watch. The only disinterested parties were at the bar, where Ace was still trying to convince the ladies that his business card photo was an accurate representation of his manhood.

Billy Normile and Johnny Alphabets were seated at the scorer's table for this momentous event. Something strange had happened to Billy over the past few weeks. He didn't know the cause, but for some reason his mojo was back. After two years of apathy he was constantly thinking about pulling off pranks.

An analysis of why this was happening would have to wait. Right now, a classic gag had hatched in his brain. This caper would take flawless timing, but if he pulled it off, the results would be epic.

Billy waited for the moment Mike slid his left foot forward to begin his approach. Billy leaned into Johnny Alphabets and whispered. "I need another beer." He pointed to a button to Johnny's right. "Do me a favor, buddy and hit the service button for the waitress."

Mike released the ball as Johnny responded, "No problem," as he pressed the button.

As Mike came out of his follow through position, his excitement grew. His ball was on the perfect path as it hooked toward the sweet spot to the right of the head pin. He sunk into a crouch, ready to leap into the air when the pins exploded.

The automatic pinsetter didn't care that Mike Galante was ten feet from a perfect game. It possessed no emotions – it simply responded to a request. When Johnny Alphabets pushed the ball return button, the pinsetter immediately went to work. The sweep bar came down and did its job of serving as a protective barrier against improperly thrown balls.

Mike's ball smashed into the sweep bar with a loud crash. The bar jumped up two feet before crashing down on the lane, the barrier now split into two pieces.

Billy's head was face down on the table as he unsuccessfully tried to hide his glee. Johnny Alphabets was baffled. He had yet to associate his push of the button with the result down the lane. "What happened?" He asked.

Billy Normile was still in no condition to respond to the inquiry.

Mike Galante was stunned. He remained in a crouch at the foul line as he stared at the broken sweep bar and his ball slowly rolling from the lane into the gutter.

Aside from Mike's shock and Johnny's confusion, there was an atmosphere of merriment among the onlookers. Suddenly, someone approached lane 28 who saw no amusement in the scene.

Gino waved his arms. "What the hell did you guys do? Do you know how much one of those pinsetters costs?"

Eddie McDaniel tried to calm the situation. "Come on, Gino, it was an accident."

"Accident my ass," Gino ranted. "Kids on Saturday afternoons pull this shit."

Eddie shrugged. "Don't get yourself so upset, Gino."

"Upset?" Gino's voice was now a high-pitched shriek. "The bar is split in half."

Mike Galante had broken free from his trance. He approached Gino and pointed to the carnage in front of the pins. "You know Gino. I've been screwed again. I'm entitled to another shot at the perfect game."

The volume of Gino's blast made the doctor proud. "OUT!" he screamed. "All of you get out, and don't come back."

"Aren't you being a bit extreme?" Mike remarked.

Gino pointed his finger directly at Mike. "And you can take your perfect game and shove it up your ass."

"Everybody out," Gino insisted as he herded the conventioneers towards the exit. When he passed the bar, he made a quick stop. "You two," he commanded, "get out!"

Ace shook his head and pointed to Willie. "We were over here the whole time, Gino. We had nothing to do with what was going on at the lane."

Gino pointed to the exit door. "I don't care. Both of you get out."

Ace and Willie got off their stools. "Well ladies, are you coming with us?" Ace asked.

The lady closest to Ace shook her head. "I don't think so. The bartender told us we still have a free drink coming."

Ace and Willie hung their heads and began to make their exit. The giggling from the bar caused Ace to turn around. One of the girls held up Ace's business card and pointed to Ace. "Look," she announced, "he doesn't have a big dick, he has a little dick."

Billy Normile held the exit door open. "Correction ladies – he has a needle dick."

Billy waved to Ace and Willie. "Come on, needle dick, let's get out of here before Gino calls 911 and we have a rematch with the NYPD."

The last thing Ace Styles heard as he moved into the stairway were the drunken shrieks from the bar of, "Goodnight, needle dick."

The group lingered on the sidewalk trying to determine their next move.

"Well, I guess that's that." Eddie McDaniel announced.

"What do you mean?" Johnny Alphabets asked.

Eddie shook his head. "The convention is history. We might as well face facts."

"Do you really think so?" Lexi added.

Billy Normile responded to her comment. "It may not be over for you and Petroni – you two just have to get a room, but where are the rest of us going to go?"

Lexi looked down to the sidewalk and bit her lip, sorry she had attempted to contribute to the conversation.

"HEY!" The volume of Doctor Dolan's shout garnered everyone's attention. "There's a pool hall near 12th Street, above the Chinese restaurant."

The other District 4 personnel shrugged and shuffled their feet after hearing the doctor's suggestion. It was Certs Eckhart who took the decisive action. "TPF, fall in on me," he commanded.

With his troops lined up behind him, Certs gave a final command. "Forward, march!"

Certs marched north toward 12th Street like a mother duck leading a parade of her ducklings. Billy Normile shrugged and looked at his 3rd platoon compatriots. "Why not?" he said.

Ace Styles and Willie Dewar brought up the rear of the procession. They were still caught up in their own conversation. "I don't know, Willie," Ace lamented. "I think the photo on my business card may be too much."

Willie shook his head vigorously. "No, no, Ace," he insisted. "Like I keep telling you, it looks great – very subtle. As a matter of fact, I think I'm gonna stuff some socks down my pants tomorrow."

"No kidding?" Ace replied. "Six socks worked for me, but you better do a little trial and error."

And so, ended another chapter in the hairbag nation.

About the Author

Robert L. Bryan is a law enforcement and security professional. He served twenty years with the New York City Transit Police and the New York City Police Department, retiring at the rank of Captain. Presently, Mr. Bryan is the Chief Security Officer for a New York State government agency. He has a B.S in criminal justice from St. John's University and an M.S. in security management from John Jay College of Criminal Justice. Additionally, Mr. Bryan is an Adjunct Professor in the Homeland Security Department and the Security Systems and Law Enforcement Technology Department for two New York Metropolitan area colleges. For more information about Mr. Bryan's other books, please visit his Amazon Author page:
https://www.amazon.com/Robert-L.-Bryan/e/B01LXUSALG?ref_=dbs_p_ebk_r00_abau_00_0000

Made in the USA
Coppell, TX
12 May 2021

55533142R00108